'I'm not sure what you mean—you seem to constantly surprise me.' David dropped his voice to a husky, throaty whisper. 'That's why I find you so intriguing. . .why I can't wait to get to know you better.'

She gave a nervous laugh. 'And I thought you'd chosen me for my professional skills, Dr Sanderson!'

'That had something to do with it. But I'm also going to need an amusing companion for my off-duty in this tropical paradise. And I hope you won't be walking around with your hair in that spinster's knot.'

Before she could stop him, he had reached down and pulled out the two strategic pins that held the chignon in place.

'There, that's better!' He ran his fingers through her hair, arranging it like a cape over the navy blue linen shoulders of her sister's uniform.

Why was David being so demonstrably affectionate? Was he trying to insinuate that their departure to Malaysia held more significance than a medical assignment warranted? Because this was news to her. . .but she had to admit she was enjoying every minute! Never in her wildest dreams had she thought David Sanderson would pay her the sort of attention she was getting now.

Margaret Barker pursued a variety of interesting careers before she became a full-time author. Besides holding a BA degree in French and Linguistics she is a Licentiate of the Royal Academy of Music, a State Registered Nurse and a qualified teacher. While living in Africa Margaret had a radio programme with the Nigerian Broadcasting Corporation. Happily married for more than thirty years, she has two sons, a daughter and an increasing number of grandchildren. Her travels in Europe, Asia, Africa and America have given Margaret the background for her foreign novels and her own teaching hospital in England has provided ideas for her Medical Romances. She lives with her husband in a sixteenth-century thatched house near the sea.

Previous Titles

LOVING CARE
FORGIVE AND FORGET
BEDSIDE MANNERS
SURGEON RIVALS

TROPICAL PARADISE

BY

MARGARET BARKER

MILLS & BOON LIMITED
ETON HOUSE   18–24 PARADISE ROAD
RICHMOND   SURREY   TW9 1SR

All the characters in this book have no existence outside the imagination of the Author, and have no relation whatsoever to anyone bearing the same name or names. They are not even distantly inspired by any individual known or unknown to the Author, and all the incidents are pure invention.

All Rights Reserved. The text of this publication or any part thereof may not be reproduced or transmitted in any form or by any means, electronic or mechanical, including photocopying, recording, storage in an information retrieval system, or otherwise, without the written permission of the publisher.

This book is sold subject to the condition that it shall not, by way of trade or otherwise, be lent, resold, hired out or otherwise circulated without the prior consent of the publisher in any form of binding or cover other than that in which it is published and without a similar condition including this condition being imposed on the subsequent purchaser.

First published in Great Britain 1991 by Mills & Boon Limited

© Margaret Barker 1991

*Australian copyright 1991
Philippine copyright 1991
This edition 1991*

ISBN 0 263 77373 6

*Set in 10 on 12 pt Linotron Palatino
03-9108-48537
Typeset in Great Britain by Centracet, Cambridge
Made and printed in Great Britain*

CHAPTER ONE

MELISSA was still reeling from the impact of David's proposal. Although when she was honest with herself she recognised that it wasn't so much a proposal as a mutually satisfying work situation. But still, David could have chosen anyone from the hospital to go with him to the tropical island of Tanu as his personal nursing assistant. And he'd chosen her!

He'd given her a couple of weeks to make her decision, and she'd played it cool and taken the full time before giving him her answer. And all that time she had hugged her secret excitement inside her, because David had asked her not to talk about it. If she had given him a negative reply he would have had to ask someone else.

She smiled to herself as she swung along the hospital corridor, thinking of the stampede of willing candidates. Most of her colleagues would have been trampled underfoot if David had made an announcement that he was looking for a competent nursing sister.

It was typical of David that he had decided to celebrate as soon as she'd told him of her decision. She remembered how his handsome face had crinkled up into a cheeky grin this morning. He'd touched her lightly under the chin, raising her face to look up at him.

'We'll make a great team out there in our tropical paradise,' he'd told her.

And it had been difficult to disguise the shiver of excitement that ran through her. Because she had been attracted to David Sanderson since the first day she met him on the wards at St Celine's. Since that first moment, when he'd asked her to help him set up an IV. She remembered how she had looked up into those dark brown eyes that could be deadly serious one minute and shimmering with mischief the next. Oh, yes, she knew only too well about his mood changes, even though he'd only asked her out a couple of times.

Why me? she thought for the umpteenth time as she ran down the rather grand, wide stone staircase towards the medical residents' quarters. And why is David making such a big fuss about the assignment? She would have been quite happy to slip quietly away next month, but oh, no! David had to do everything in style. Since her acceptance this morning he had arranged an impromptu party.

'I won't have time to change,' she'd told him. 'I'm on duty till nine tonight.'

'Ever heard of a come-as-you-are party?' he'd asked her laughingly.

She could hear the noise of the revellers all the way down the staircase. It would be a wonder if someone didn't come to complain! Along the corridor she could see the door to David's room was wide open. Hastily she pulled off her white, frilly sister's cap and felt at the coiled chignon on the top of her red hair. She had plaited it and secured it neatly hours ago. It wasn't exactly party-style, but there was no time to change it now.

'And about time too!' David came towards her, a glass of wine in his hand. 'What kept you?'

She smiled. 'Some of us have to keep the hospital going. David! I wanted to ask you about the newly admitted cholecystectomy. You haven't written up the. . .'

'This is a party, Melissa. The patient isn't going down to Theatre for a couple of days, so what's the rush? I'll see her in the morning.'

'But she's asking for something to help her sleep,' Melissa persisted.

David frowned. 'Rule number one: learn the art of delegation.' He turned round and called across the room. 'Richard!'

The young houseman came running. 'Yes, sir?'

David smiled. 'Nip up to Sister Goldsbrough's ward and write up the new cholecystectomy patient for a sedative. I checked her out in Outpatients yesterday. Temazepam should be suitable.'

Melissa found herself smiling as she accepted the glass of wine. 'I hope you're not going to expect the same blind obedience from me,' she remarked.

He laughed. 'I'm not sure what I expect from you, Melissa. You constantly surprise me.' He dropped his voice to a husky, throaty whisper. 'That's why I find you so intriguing. . .why I can't wait to get to know you better.'

She gave a nervous laugh. 'And I thought you'd chosen me for my professional skills, Dr Sanderson!'

'That had something to do with it. But I'm also

going to need an amusing companion for my off-duty in this tropical paradise. And I hope you won't be walking around with your hair in that spinster's knot.'

Before she could stop him, he had reached down and pulled out the two strategic pins that held the chignon in place. As the plait fell down over her shoulders, he deftly began to unwind it, his fingers relentlessly pulling out the long, red, imprisoned strands.

'There, that's better!' He ran his fingers through her hair, arranging it like a cape over the navy blue linen shoulders of her sister's uniform.

She felt her heart thumping and she was terribly aware of the eyes of her medical colleagues. Why was David being so demonstrably affectionate? Was he trying to insinuate that their departure to Malaysia held more significance than a medical assignment warranted? Because this was news to her. . .but she had to admit she was enjoying every minute! Never in her wildest dreams had she thought David Sanderson would pay her the sort of attention she was getting now.

She looked around the room, sensing the envious eyes of some of her female colleagues. David was, without doubt, the heart-throb of the hospital. And she was taking him away from all this. It was too good to be true.

She experienced a tiny pang of apprehension. There had to be a catch in it somewhere. Maybe she would wake up and find it had all been a dream. Or perhaps she would have to pay for her new-found happiness later.

She took a sip of her wine, telling herself that was negative thinking. That was the old Melissa trying to get through again. The child Melissa whom nobody wanted, who had learned early in life that it was best to expect nothing from life. That way, you didn't get hurt. But in the last few years, since she had taken charge of her life in adulthood, she'd found that you could have anything you wanted if you really went for it. And she was certainly going to go for David Sanderson...but in a subtle way! There was no point in capitulating all at once.

She could feel his hand under her arm and allowed herself to be steered among the crush of people.

'Marvellous news, Sister! Wish we could all come with you!' said one of her staff nurses.

'Glad you can't!' quipped David, putting an arm around Melissa's shoulders in a proprietorial way. 'It's only a tiny island. We're going to play at Robinson Crusoe.'

'Some people have all the luck,' said a seductive female voice.

Melissa felt David stiffen as they both turned to look at the woman in the doorway.

'Well, aren't you going to ask me in, David?' the woman asked in a low, throaty whisper, that was barely audible above the general cacophony.

Melissa had recognised the newcomer at once, although her erstwhile nursing colleague appeared to have aged considerably in the four years since she had left the hospital.

'Jenny it's good to see you again. Marriage seems to suit you,' lied Melissa, reaching out her hands in a gesture of welcome.

But David was holding her back, his hand under her elbow restraining her.

'I wasn't aware that you'd been invited, Jenny,' he said icily.

The unwelcome guest gave a hoarse laugh. 'Since when did I need an invitation from you, David? Time was when you. . .'

'That's enough, Jenny!' David took a step forward, adopting a menacing stance. 'I'm asking you to leave.'

Melissa squirmed with embarrassment. As she looked at Jenny, she remembered only how kind and helpful this ex-sister had been to her when she first came to St Celine's. Four years older than herself, Jenny had often been the one Melissa had turned to for advice, and she had never been disappointed. And she had made a point of not joining in the speculation that had surrounded Jenny's abrupt resignation from the hospital. She remembered hearing that Jenny was pregnant, but her immediate marriage to a wealthy company director had silenced all further gossip. The general consensus of opinion had been that Jenny Linden had done well for herself, and all further interest had been stemmed. A few months later, Melissa remembered hearing that Jenny had given birth to a baby boy. She had sent a congratulations card, but there had been no reply.

Firmly, Melissa removed David's hand from her arm and moved towards Jenny.

'I don't know what this is all about, Jenny, but maybe you'd better go. You know what David's like when he's in a bad mood,' she added almost under her breath.

Jenny gave a brittle smile. 'Oh, I know what David's like probably better than you, my dear, which is why I'm here.'

Melissa glanced nervously around and noted that David had returned to his guests at the other end of the room. Already, the charming smile had lightened up his face and he appeared to have forgotten the embarrassing incident.

Melissa frowned. 'I don't understand, Jenny. What are you trying to tell me?'

Jenny reached out a hand and pulled her out into the corridor. Leaning against the wall, she spoke quickly, through clenched teeth.

'David Sanderson is a philandering womaniser. If you go anywhere with him you're in for trouble. I don't want you to make the same mistake that I did. That's why I had to come here tonight, to warn you.'

Melissa frowned. 'Warn me about what?'

Jenny's eyes flashed. 'We can't talk here. Come and see me at home.' She fished a card from her bag and pressed it into Melissa's palm. 'Come during the day when my husband will be out. . .any afternoon this week would be a good time. My son goes out for a walk with his nanny in the afternoons and we can talk in peace.'

Melissa glanced briefly at the card, noting the West London address.

'But surely. . .' she began, but her words were obliterated in the sudden clanging of the emergency bell ringing above their heads in the corridor. She clapped her hands over her ears. The sound always induced a *frisson* of terror into her, reminding her so vividly of her unhappy childhood, and it was some seconds before she was totally in command of herself again. This was something she had had to learn to control over her years in the medical world. She mustn't go to pieces now when every aspect of her medical expertise would be required.

Jenny's face held a mocking smile. 'Nothing changes here,' she mouthed, as she made to move away.

'Wait!' Melissa called, but her voice was drowned in the cacophony of bells and stamping feet. Out of the corner of her eye she could see David bearing down upon her, followed behind by the other medics.

'Accident and Emergency!' His raised voice was suddenly audible as the bells stopped ringing. He glanced briefly at the departing figure of Jenny before taking hold of Melissa by the shoulders, his dark brown eyes boring deep inside her.

'Whatever she told you is untrue. The woman was always an inveterate liar and a troublemaker. I forbid you to see her again, Melissa.'

Melissa wriggled out of his grasp and glared up into his eyes. 'Forbid is not a word you should use with me. I'm a free agent and don't you forget it! You may be the director in charge of this tropical project, but don't think that means you can order what I should do with my private life.'

For a moment she thought he was going to strike her. His handsome face had tensed into a harsh mask, and she realised that she knew nothing at all about this high-powered, ambitious man. And yet she was preparing to go halfway round the world with him, knowing that they would be thrown together in situations far more demanding than anything that could happen in this high-tech, well-staffed hospital.

His arms dropped to his sides in a gesture of resignation.

'We have to go now; there's a full-scale emergency on our hands.'

She followed his lean, athletic figure as he bounded up the stairs, two at a time. He didn't turn around to see if she was still with him, and it was some time before she caught up with him again in Accident and Emergency. As she ran up the stairs, she wound her hair back into a practical knot and stuffed it into her cap. A couple of spare pins from her pocket secured it firmly, and no one who saw her walking into Accident and Emergency would have dreamed that this cool, poised sister had recently had her hair tumbled about her shoulders by the tall, distinguished doctor who was taking charge of the difficult medical situation.

Melissa approached the sister of Accident and Emergency, anxious to be put in the picture. It appeared there had been a collision between two trains and all London hospitals were on full alert. Even as they discussed the emergency, the first casualties started to arrive.

They had to deal first with the seriously injured whose lives were in danger. An SOS for more blood and plasma was sent out and donors began to arrive. Melissa cordoned off a special section for the haematology unit.

'How many beds empty on your ward, Sister Goldsbrough?' David called from across the room.

Melissa did a rapid calculation. 'Six, when I went off duty.'

'Go and see if you can put some of the convalescent patients into the day-room. You've got to take at least ten orthopaedic cases,' he replied brusquely.

'Male or female?' she asked mechanically.

David ran a hand through his dark hair in a gesture of impatience. 'Does it matter, woman?'

Melissa drew in her breath and forced herself to restrain the response that hovered on her lips. David was bearing the brunt of the organisation of the emergency. She mustn't make his task any harder. She noticed how he was always the master of improvisation—in fact, he seemed to thrive on situations that were out of the ordinary. Perhaps that was why he'd taken on the challenging post in Malaysia. But why had *she* taken it on?

As she hurried away from the organised chaos of Accident and Emergency a little voice inside her head was whispering the truth.

Most of the patients on her ward were awake. The ringing of the bells, the noise of tramping feet and the swinging of the doors as trolleys were wheeled in had made all but the most deeply sedated patients sit up and watch what was going on.

The young night staff nurse in charge of the ward turned as Melissa walked in, and a smile of relief broke out over her face.

'Oh, Sister, thank goodness you're here! I've been trying to get hold of one of the night sisters. This new orthopaedic case is written up for morphine, but I need someone to check it for me. And we haven't got a bed. Where am I going to put her?'

'Keep calm, Nurse,' said Melissa briskly, recognising the beginning of panic rising in the girl. She would make an excellent sister later on if she could control her emotions. Melissa knew that, academically, the staff nurse had always been near the top of her class, but she sometimes found it hard to cope with unforeseen situations.

Rather like me, on both counts, Melissa thought reflectively, as she reached for the key to the poisons cupboard. Her nursing exams had proved no problem; she had always enjoyed studying. It was applying the knowledge she'd absorbed to the practical medical situations that she had found most difficult.

Melissa bent over the prostrate figure of their patient, noting the tense, drawn, haggard look of pain on the young woman's face. The diagnosis of fracture of the left femur had been made before she arrived at the ward and she would need to go to Theatre as soon as it was possible. She glanced at the notes as she drew the morphine up into a syringe. Fiona Smith, age eighteen; travelling with fiancé, now in Intensive Care.

'How's Brian?' the girl whispered as Melissa gave her the injection.

Melissa gave her patient a gentle smile. 'Your fiancé?'

'We're getting married on Saturday,' the girl replied in a deadpan voice.

Melissa swallowed. 'He's in the hospital, Fiona, but I'll have to check on his condition for you. It may take some time, as we're rather busy, but I'll get back to you as soon as I can.'

The young patient nodded resignedly, and closed her eyes.

Melissa hurried down the ward and approached the beds nearest the day-room. There were four post-operative patients, soon to be discharged, who wouldn't come to any harm if they were asked to spend a few hours in the reclining armchairs.

'Just until we've sorted out the bed situation, you understand,' she told them, with an encouraging smile.

'Of course, Sister,' said the oldest of the four, a round-faced motherly woman with soft grey hair, who held a high opinion of Sister Goldsbrough. 'It's just like during the war, isn't it? All hands on deck. . .'

Melissa was aware of a tall figure waiting impatiently beside her.

'When you've finished the chat, perhaps you could give me a hand in Theatre. We've opened up the two disused theatres and we need a couple more surgical teams. I've volunteered to take charge of one and appointed you as my theatre sister. Staff Nurse can cope here now you've sorted out the bed situation.'

Melissa stared up at David. 'I haven't done any theatre work for a couple of years.'

'Then it's time you got into practice again, because heaven knows what surgery we'll have to cope with when we get out to Malaysia.'

CHAPTER TWO

MELISSA pulled off her surgical mask as she walked out of the operating theatre. One of the off-duty theatre sisters had just arrived and insisted on taking over from her.

She realised that she'd lost all count of time as she and David had worked on through the night. It had been a relief to find that her early training in surgical technique had stood her in good stead. And David had been his usual efficient self, seemingly tireless as he coped with the steady influx of injured patients.

She had found it something of a strain to operate on the young girl, Fiona Smith, the fractured femur from her own ward. Before being given the anaesthetic Fiona had been drowsily rambling about her church wedding, due to take place in four days' time. It had been all Melissa could do to prevent the tears from welling up in her eyes. She knew she shouldn't become emotionally involved with her patient, but it was so difficult not to empathise with her.

When the girl was fully anaesthetised on the operating table, Melissa had assisted David to fix a Steinmann's pin behind the tibial tubercule, which enabled them to apply a Thomas's splint with a Pearson's knee flexion piece on which to rest the limb. She knew that skeletal balanced traction over a period of time would ensure immobilisation and allow the mid-shaft fracture of the femur to heal. . .but not in time for a wedding on Saturday!

Now, as she glanced out through the corridor window, she was surprised to see the first rosy glow that heralded the dawn surrounding the top of the hospital roof. Where had the night gone to? It seemed only minutes since she was downstairs in David's room. And yet so much had happened.

'Tired, Melissa?'

She looked up as she recognised the familiar voice. David had caught up with her, without her noticing.

She smiled wearily. 'I think I must be, because I didn't hear you coming up behind me. All my faculties are going into a decline.'

'Time you switched off, then,' he told her, in a gentle voice. 'How about a nightcap down in my room?'

She could feel her pulses racing. 'Sounds like a good idea, but what about all the work? We can't just abandon the situation at this stage.'

'Everything's under control. We've mustered a positive army of auxiliary nurses during the night, and a new batch of off-duty medics has just arrived. Besides, we're not much use to the patients in this stage. Far better for us to get some rest, so we can live to fight another day.'

Melissa smiled, allowing her weary legs to propel her onwards as if on automatic pilot. 'When you put it like that, I don't need any persuading! But first I have to go back to my ward to see Fiona Smith, our fractured femur. I've just rung down to Intensive

Care to ask about her fiancé. They're supposed to be getting married on Saturday.'

'Is he called Brian Davis? Head and chest injuries?' Melissa nodded. 'I remember admitting him. How is he now?'

'Sister says there's little change in his condition, but he seems to be holding his own. He's basically a healthy young man.'

'Let's hope he pulls through.' David paused by the door of Melissa's ward. 'Go in and deliver your message. I'll wait here, otherwise I'll be besieged with more work.'

Melissa spent a couple of minutes in the ward talking to her night staff nurse. It appeared that her patient, Fiona Smith, was still not completely round from the anaesthetic. Melissa went to see her patient to check on her condition. Satisfying herself that all was well, she asked the staff nurse to be suitably sympathetic when she reported on Brian Davis's condition.

David put an arm loosely around Melissa's shoulders as they began the descent into the residents' quarters.

His room bore all the evidence of the recently curtailed party, and he grimaced. 'What a mess!'

'I'll help you clear up,' said Melissa, picking up a couple of glasses.

'Oh, no, you won't! This can wait until later. I've got a much better idea. Let's clear a space on the sofa so that you can put your feet up. Doctor's orders!'

She grinned as she spread herself indulgently

amid the debris, tossing a couple of medical magazines on to the littered floor. 'I'm not complaining at the treatment. What else do you prescribe, Doctor?'

'How about a brandy?'

'If you insist.'

'I do.' He joined her on the sofa, a couple of crystal glasses in his hand.

She took a sip of her brandy and the warm glow began to revive her flagging energy. 'It's a strange profession, isn't it?' she remarked.

David gave a dry laugh. 'It's a bit late to have second thoughts about it now.'

'Oh, I'm not having second thoughts,' she said hurriedly. 'I wouldn't want to do anything else.'

'Neither would I, so we're going to make a good team, you and I.'

He reached forward and took the brandy glass from her hand, placing it carefully on a low wooden table.

Melissa was aware of the scent of his aftershave, mingled with the indefinable odour of various medical concoctions that had impregnated themselves into his skin.

She giggled, 'You smell like a chemist's shop!'

He threw back his head and laughed. 'You're so romantic, Melissa.'

Her heart was thumping too loudly and she was sure David would try to make some witty medical comment. 'I didn't know this was meant to be a romantic occasion,' she said quickly.

He leaned forward and before she could move he had scooped her into his arms, his mouth dangerously close to hers as he whispered, 'You don't think I invited you down here to talk shop, do you?'

'I'm not sure what. . .' she began, but his lips came down hungrily on hers.

As she closed her eyes to savour the delicious moment, a sudden fleeting glimpse of Jenny's anguished face appeared in her mind. And again she heard her friend's damning accusation. 'David is a philandering womaniser. . . I don't want what happened to me to happen to you.'

For a second she struggled in David's arms, but he barely seemed to notice, or if he did, he must have thought she was putting on an act. His hands were gently caressing her, pulling her ever closer into his embrace. She found it impossible to ignore the tantalising sensations that began to sweep over her. She felt her body go limp with desire as his lips moved over her face, kissing her gently over and over again until all she wanted to do was to surrender her whole body to this exciting, stimulating, sensual man.

'Wait!' Was that really her own voice? Had she somehow summoned the strength to reject his passionate advances?

'What's the matter?' he asked, in a deep, throaty, seductive voice.

She looked up into his dark eyes and saw only tenderness. He had never kissed her with such passion before and she had never responded like this. . .never intimated that they might become lovers. On the couple of occasions when they'd gone out together, the evening had ended with a friendly peck on the cheek.

'I don't know you, David,' she murmured haltingly. 'We're total strangers.'

He smiled down at her. 'And likely to stay that way, if you insist on calling a halt just when we're getting to know each other. . .did anyone ever tell you, you've got the most amazingly beautiful eyes? I can't decide whether they're green or almond, but they're totally unique.'

Melissa struggled to sit up, running a hand distractedly through her tousled hair. 'David, we've got to talk.'

'That sounds ominous.' He moved to the edge of the sofa and took a sip of his brandy. 'Any subject in particular?'

'It was Jenny. . .something she said tonight.'

'Ah—I thought that might be the problem. She's spreading rumours about me again, is she?'

'Is there any truth in what she says?' Melissa asked directly.

His eyes flashed angrily as he faced her again. 'Depends on what she's trumped up this time, doesn't it? What did she tell you?'

'Nothing specific. . .but she intimated that. . .'

'Nothing specific! Vague lies again!' He stood up and began to pace the room. 'You mustn't listen to her, Melissa. I want us to have a special relationship when we leave this hospital. A relationship based on mutual trust. . .do you understand me?'

She heard the distress in his voice and for a moment she felt sorry for his predicament. Maybe he and Jenny had quarrelled about something and Jenny was trying to get back at him by spreading vicious rumours. On the other hand, there might be some truth. There was no smoke without fire. How many other women had David brought down to this room to play out the big seduction scene? Perhaps Jenny knew what she was talking about. Well, there was only one way to find out.

She stood up determinedly. 'I've got to go; it's late.' How trite the words sounded, even to her own ears.

David gave her a wry grin, seeming to regain some of his suave composure again. 'Or early, whichever way you look at it.'

He walked over to the door and flung it wide open. 'Forgive me if I don't escort you back to the Virgins' Retreat. I'm sure you'll come to no harm. Just keep a tight hold on the key of your chastity belt and you'll be quite safe.'

Melissa thought he seemed relieved when she went out into the corridor. There was no attempt at a goodbye kiss, just a casual wave of his hand as he closed the door.

She hurried away up the stone staircase into the main body of the hospital. Not until she was going up in the lift to the sisters' rooms on the top floor did she take a deep breath and review the situation. It had been a mistake to challenge David about Jenny. It was obviously something about which he felt very strongly. And until she had seen Jenny and heard what she had to say there was no point in pursuing the matter.

She stepped out of the lift and made for her room at the end of the corridor. As she let herself in, her eyes strayed across to the window. It was daylight; outside, the familiar early-morning sights and sounds of London greeted her. A new day had dawned while she had been cloistered with David.

A new day in which she was going to find out the truth about the man she planned to go away with.

After a few hours' sleep Melissa got herself back on to the ward by the middle of the morning. Her daytime charge nurse was doing the rounds with one of the consultants and was relieved to let Melissa take over. The consultant agreed to discharge the four post-operative patients who had been consigned to the day-room, on condition they return for daily treatment in Outpatients.

When the consultant had gone, Melissa organised the team of auxiliary nurses who had taken over some of the simpler tasks from the trained staff. It seemed the emergency situation caused by the train crash was under control. Every bed in the hospital was full, but the trained staff, aided by various volunteer groups, were coping admirably.

At the end of the morning Melissa made time to go and have a chat with Fiona Smith.

'How's the leg feeling, Fiona?' she asked.

The young patient gave a wry smile. 'Don't ask, Sister! I'm pretending it doesn't belong to me.'

Melissa smiled back into the girl's brave face, before turning to adjust the pads on the Thomas's splint.

'That better?' she asked gently.

'Mm, I think it is,' Fiona said cautiously. 'Any more news of Brian?'

'I just rang down to Intensive Care. I'm afraid there's no change in his condition,' Melissa replied softly. 'But it's early days. He's basically a healthy young man, so the news should get better.'

The girl's eyes filled with tears. 'When my mum comes, I suppose I'd better tell her to cancel the wedding,' she sighed.

Melissa put her hand over the patient's. 'Not cancel, Fiona, just postpone it.' She was praying inside that she wasn't raising false hopes.

The patient brightened. 'Yes, you're right, Sister. Just postpone it. Or maybe we could get married in hospital. People do, don't they?'

'Well, sometimes,' Melissa admitted cautiously.

'Could you arrange it, Sister?' the patient persisted.

Melissa took a deep breath. 'I really can't promise anything at this stage, Fiona—there are too many things to take into consideration. Let's see how things work out, shall we?'

'How long do legs take to mend?' Fiona asked earnestly.

Melissa smiled. 'Good question. That depends on the patient, but you look healthy enough. A few weeks, perhaps. . .look, I've got to go now. I'll see you later.'

She moved away. It was always difficult to give accurate prognoses to orthopaedic patients. You had to steer a delicate line between raising false hopes and dampening down much-needed optimistic spirits.

Out of the corner of her eye Melissa was aware of a flutter of excitement by the ward door. Her charge nurse was adjusting her cap and nudging one of the staff nurses. As David swept into the ward, she felt her legs go weak. The contretemps last night hadn't changed her feelings for him.

He strode swiftly down the ward, making an obvious beeline for her. For an instant she felt rooted to the spot, and then her professional training took over.

'Good morning, Dr Sanderson,' she said, as he drew level with her.

'Good morning, Sister Goldsbrough. I'd like a word in the privacy of your office, if you don't mind.'

'Of course.'

David's face was so deadly serious that she had a sudden desire to burst out laughing. Whenever he wanted coffee he usually used the same ploy, and she was quite sure this was what he was after at the moment.

'I wasn't wrong,' she told him as, duly ensconced in her tiny little office at the end of the ward, she poured out a generous mugful. 'I knew your visit wasn't important.'

'Ah, but it was. I came to apologise for upsetting you last night. To make amends, I'd like to take you out this afternoon. I know you've got a two-five because I checked the off-duty board.'

Melissa pretended to busy herself with the coffee percolator as she struggled to come up with an answer. It was true she was off from two till five, but those three precious hours were going to be used to find out if there was any truth in Jenny's accusations.

'Sorry, I can't make it this afternoon, David. Prior engagement.' She sat down in her chair so that the desk was placed between the two of them, giving her the required space she felt she needed at this precise moment in time.

His dark brown, seductive eyes narrowed. 'Can't you cancel it? After all, you said yourself that we need to get to know each other. We're going to be thrown together an awful lot out in the depths of Malaysia. Supposing we're incompatible?'

She felt relieved when she saw the cheeky grin that spread across his ruggedly handsome face as he added this last remark.

'I'd love to get to know you before we go out to Malaysia, David. We've got a whole month before we leave, so if you give me a little more warning the next time, I'll make a point of being available. And now I really must get back to the ward. Help yourself to coffee.'

Her heart was fluttering as she pushed past him and went back to her duties. It had taken a great deal of determination not to weaken. Ever since she'd first met David, she had longed for him to take notice of her. And now that she had all his attention she was turning him away!

But not for long, she told herself as she swept down the ward. When she'd heard what Jenny had to say this afternoon, that would put paid to her unpleasant speculation. She would find that it had all been a mistake.

Melissa took the Tube out to West London. Although she only went a few stops, the tree-lined street that greeted her when she emerged from the depths of the Underground seemed light years removed from the hustle and bustle of central London. The traffic was slower and not so congested; mothers with babies in push-chairs stopped to chat in the middle of the pavement as if time were not the desperate commodity it was rated in the big city.

She stopped outside the station and bought some flowers from a comfortably plump, smiling lady, who put the money into the wide pocket of her capacious apron.

'You like spring flowers, do you, dear?' asked the flower lady, adding a touch of greenery to the daffodils and tulips.

Melissa smiled. 'Yes, I do, but these are for a friend. . .a special friend I lost touch with over the years.' She couldn't think why she'd confided in the older woman. Maybe it was the warm smile on her wrinkled face.

'It's sad when that happens, but she'll forgive you when she sees my daffs. Enjoy yourself, dearie; you're only young once.'

That's true, Melissa thought as she moved on down the street. So I'd better not make a mistake with David Sanderson. She glanced down at the address on Jenny's card. It was a road that led off this main street.

She turned the corner and found herself in a salubrious tree-lined avenue of solid Victorian detached houses. Halfway down the road she found Jenny's house, set well back from the road, the front door approached by a circular gravel drive. There were crocuses and primroses in well-tended beds surrounding the lush green lawn. A gardener paused to lean on his spade and watch as she rang the door-bell at the side of the rich mahogany door.

Jenny's face lit up with a warm smile as she opened the door. 'Oh, how clever of you to come to see me so promptly. . .and what lovely flowers!'

Melissa found herself in a high-ceilinged hall, the walls covered with family portraits.

'Victor's family,' said Jenny with a grin as she waved an arm dismissively towards the pictures. 'It's been like this ever since I married him. He's completely set in his ways, but then he's so much older than me. Come through into the sitting-room. We can't talk here, too many flapping ears.'

Even as Jenny was speaking, Melissa caught a glimpse of a woman looking down from the landing up above.

'You can bring some tea, Mrs Barnes,' Jenny called imperiously, before closing the sitting-room door. 'That's our housekeeper. She used to be a maid here, and Victor promoted her when we got married. She's terribly nosy, so don't talk when she brings in the tea.'

Melissa sat down in the comfortable, chintz-covered armchair which Jenny had indicated and looked across at her friend, who was now sprawled across an antique chaise-longue.

'Jenny, I haven't much time, so we'd better come to the point. What did you mean when you said that David. . .'

'I wanted to warn you not to trust him,' Jenny broke in breathlessly. 'He can't be trusted, and you simply mustn't go away with him. If I'd known what I know about him I wouldn't have been in this mess.'

Melissa glanced quickly around her at the affluent

surroundings. 'I'd hardly call this a mess! You seem to have everything you could possibly want.'

Jenny gave a harsh laugh. 'That's how it would appear. . .but David let me down four years ago. We were lovers; he said he wanted to marry me. When I told him I was pregnant, he didn't want to know.'

Melissa sat forward in her chair, her heart beating rapidly. 'You were expecting David's child?'

She broke off abruptly as the old housekeeper came into the room, carrying a silver tray, set with a delicate china tea service. But it was the little boy who was tagging along behind who intrigued Melissa—a little boy with dark hair and deep brown eyes.

'This is my son, Paul,' Jenny said evenly. 'He's going for a walk with his nanny, aren't you, Paul?'

The little boy ignored his mother and went across the room to stare up at Melissa.

Oh, those eyes! she thought, with a shiver of apprehension.

'Who are you?' the boy asked.

'I'm Melissa. Your mother and I used to work together in hospital.'

'Ah, those were the days!' Jenny said nostalgically. 'If only I could turn the clock back. . .look, here's Nanny, Paul, my darling.'

The little boy gave his mother a dutiful kiss before he ran out of the room and put his hand trustingly into that of the tall, dour, uniformed woman waiting in the hall.

'That will be all, Mrs Barnes,' Jenny said pointedly,

as the housekeeper lingered on after pouring out the tea. 'And please close the door on your way out.'

As soon as they were alone again, Jenny stood up and started pacing the room. 'As I was saying, David cast me off as soon as he knew I was pregnant. I didn't know which way to turn. I knew my parents would be heartbroken...my father's a viçar, you know, in a very narrow-minded rural community. So I decided to accept Victor's proposal. He's been a friend of the family for as long as I can remember, and he's always been fond of me; he'd been a widower for a couple of years at the time, and I knew I only had to prompt him into asking me.'

'Jenny, I'd no idea!' Melissa stared across at her friend. 'So your son...'

'Yes, Paul is David's child. Didn't you see the resemblance?'

Melissa drew in her breath, not trusting herself to reply. The resemblance had been uncanny, even in a three-year-old. But yet she still didn't want to believe it. She was clutching at straws, but there had to be some mistake. She looked again at her blonde, blue-eyed friend. The boy certainly didn't take after his mother.

'Your husband...does he resemble Paul in any way?' she asked tentatively.

'Victor?' Jenny laughed. 'He's as bald as a coot, but the bits around the side that aren't grey and the hairs on his chest are very fair. And he's got blue eyes too.'

Melissa's heart sank. 'But doesn't he suspect that Paul isn't his child?'

'He doesn't have to suspect. He was under no

illusions when we were married. I told him everything. Ours isn't a romantic marriage, Melissa, it's a marriage of convenience. He wanted a wife to run his home; I wanted a father for my child. It's as simple as that.'

Jenny broke off as the sound of tyres scrunching on the gravel drive came through the wide bay windows.

The expression on Jenny's face turned to pure panic. 'Oh, lord, Victor's home early! Look, you'd better go, Melissa. He doesn't like me having my old hospital friends out here.'

Melissa stood up, almost upsetting the china cup, delicately poised at the edge of the Sheraton table beside her.

Jenny had already flown over to the door and was ushering her out into the hall. 'It's because I care what happens to you that I've told you my secret,' she said quietly.

'Thanks, I appreciate your concern. Goodbye, Jenny.'

Melissa tried to look unconcerned as she sauntered down the front steps. Out of the corner of her eye she could see that the tall, portly man getting out of the car was watching her. Surely it would be good manners to pause and greet him. . .but no! Jenny had fixed her with a look that told her to go quickly.

'Just someone trying to give me a catalogue, dear,' she heard Jenny say, as she walked off down towards the road.

She took a deep breath as she reached the main street. The glimpse of Jenny's husband had confirmed the fact that he bore no resemblance to the dear little boy with the wide brown eyes and the mischievous smile she had seen so often on someone else.

She stopped dead in her tracks as she saw the dark blue Mercedes cruise to a halt beside her.

David pushed open the passenger door. 'Get in!'

She heard his ominous tone and her legs felt weak. 'I came out here on the Tube and I'm quite capable of. . .'

'Don't argue, woman!' He wrenched open his door and swung round the front of the car to stand beside her, glaring down in a menacing fashion. 'I knew this was where you'd be. You couldn't trust me, could you? You had to go digging up the dirt. . . look, we can't discuss it here!' He held the passenger door, staring down at her angrily.

Melissa hesitated and looked around her. Several of the passersby were beginning to give her curious looks. Quickly she stepped into the car and sank back against the leather seat, her heart thumping wildly.

CHAPTER THREE

NEITHER of them spoke during the journey back to the hospital. Melissa was dimly aware of David's angry figure crouched over the steering-wheel, but she kept her face turned to the window. Outside, the blur of sedate family houses changed to taller buildings, hotels and offices as the car went towards central London. David carved his way through the dense traffic at Hyde Park Corner and eased the Mercedes along beside Buckingham Palace. Melissa glanced automatically at the flagpole as they passed the fountains; she noted that the flag was flying to indicate that the Queen was at home.

The inconsequential thought had barely had time to register before they were driving along beside Green Park; there was more congestion near to Westminster Abbey. She thought how imposing the old Abbey looked in the early evening sunlight as she desperately tried to forget her own problems.

This monster of a man, who had somehow managed to captivate her heart, so that she couldn't think straight, was going to have some explaining to do when they got back to the hospital! He'd no right to ride roughshod over her like this and insinuate that she was in the wrong, simply because she'd tried to find out the truth.

But she remained silent in the car; it wouldn't be safe in all this traffic to challenge him now. They were hurtling along the Embankment, and she looked out at the sun shining on the river Thames. In a few minutes they would be back at hospital. . .and then the confrontation could begin!

As David brought the car to a halt in front of the main door of the hospital, she put a hand on the passenger seat door, but he leaned across and prevented her opening it.

'Just a minute, Melissa. We need to talk.'

She was aware of the power of his strong, muscular body as he remained with his hand over hers on the door, his eyes boring menacingly inside her. And she recognised that even now, in this unpleasant situation, she couldn't help feeling a *frisson* of excitement at the nearness of him. It was as if the man exuded physical sexuality; she didn't blame Jenny for falling for him, but she would blame herself for the rest of her life if she allowed herself to fall blindly under his spell.

She moved her hand from beneath his and sank back against the soft leather of the seat. 'Yes, we do need to talk,' she said carefully, glancing out of the window at the crush of ambulances and cars. 'But not here. What I have to say must be said in private.'

She glanced at her watch. David's lift back to hospital had saved her some time, but she still had to be back on duty for the evening.

'What I have to say can be said anywhere,' David retorted. 'Jenny's been spreading lies about me ever since she left hospital, so there's nothing new in the situation. But we'll go to my room if it'll make you feel any easier.'

She watched him easing himself out of the car and

waited until he had come round the front and opened her door. Deliberately pulling herself to her full height and trying to regain all her composure, she followed him into the hospital and down into the residents' quarters.

The cleaners must have been in and set everything to rights again, because there was no sign of the debris from the party. There was even a bunch of daffodils on the coffee-table. Melissa glanced at the card poised beside it and recognised the sender. It was from one of the sisters who had been at the party, and the brief message was that it had been a pity the party had broken up so soon.

'Another grateful admirer,' she said in a brittle voice as she sank down on the sofa.

David's thundercloud face relaxed for the first time since he had picked her up in the car. 'Can I help it if I'm irresistible to women?' he quipped, with a wry grin.

'You love playing the Don Juan, don't you?' She had tried, unsuccessfully, to keep the rancour out of her voice.

He laughed. 'I do believe you're jealous, Melissa.'

'No, I'm not!'

'Methinks the lady doth protest too much.' He spread an arm along the back of the sofa, almost touching her shoulder.

She receded to the corner of the sofa as if he had struck her. 'Let's get one thing straight, David. Our relationship is purely professional. I have no hold on you, you have no hold on me. But when it comes to my friends. . .when I hear that you've actually made a girl pregnant and then absolved all responsibility. . .'

'Oh, that old story! I wondered which version she'd told you. You surely don't believe Jenny, do you?'

Melissa was taken aback by his bantering tone. She had expected fireworks, not this suddenly calm situation. Looking across the sofa at David, she could swear that his eyes were twinkling with amusement.

'Then you deny everything?' she asked falteringly.

He moved towards her, suddenly cupping her chin in his hands, tilting her face upwards so that she could see his unflickering eyes. 'Of course I do,' he told her softly.

She continued to look up into his deep brown, expressive eyes and saw what looked like sincerity. But then those dark eyes reminded her of the little boy's unflinching stare.

She moved her head to one side, unable to bear the powerful scrutiny. 'But Jenny's son is dark-haired and brown-eyed. . .unlike both his parents,' she persisted.

David gave an exasperated sigh. 'And I thought you were a scientific person! Didn't you do any genetics during your training?'

'Elementary genetics, yes,' she said cautiously.

He gave her a broad, patronising smile. 'But not enough to equip you to make sound judgements on parentage. Otherwise you'd know that many children are genetic throwbacks to previous generations. Obviously Jenny or her husband must have some dark forebears.'

Melissa gave a deep sigh as she felt some of the

tension easing out of her. 'Put like that, it seems perfectly feasible,' she admitted.

He frowned. 'You're still not convinced, are you? Melissa, the most worrying aspect of this is the fact that you don't trust me. And if you can't trust me, then I'd rather you didn't come out to Malaysia with me. I can easily replace you, so if you'd rather opt out now, it would make it easier for everyone.'

She drew in her breath as she looked up again into those dark searching eyes. A feeling of panic was rising up inside her. She wanted to go away with David on this assignment more than anything else in the world. It had been like a dream come true when he had selected her. She had to believe him. . .she must take him at his word.

She smiled with a confidence she didn't feel. 'I trust you, David,' she said softly, and found that just by saying the words she could make herself believe them.

'That's my girl! You won't regret your decision, I promise you. It's going to be a wonderful experience for both of us. . .it's the chance of a lifetime. Who knows where it will lead us, professionally!'

She heard the excitement in his voice and found herself being swept along by his enthusiasm.

'What exactly is the set-up out there?' she asked.

David smiled happily, leaning back expansively against the sofa, his arm casually draped along the back so that his fingers brushed lightly against her arm.

'It's a completely new medical project. An international consortium of businessmen, mainly from London, Kuala Lumpur and Singapore, is financing the development of a holiday retreat on the beautiful, undeveloped tropical island of Tanu off the east coast of Malaysia. To this holiday paradise they're going to send their stressed executives and their families, post-operative and convalescent patients, personnel with dietary disorders and others who simply need a holiday away from the cares of civilisation. The visitors will be housed in ethnic cabins with thatched roofs to give them the impression of being in an unspoiled tropical paradise.'

'Sounds wonderful! But what about the native people on the island? Are they happy to be invaded?'

'There are only a few people living on the island, and the consortium has agreed to give free medical treatment to any of them who require it. Apparently the indigenous population are very happy about this, because formerly they had to travel to the mainland, and the journey can be difficult if the sea is rough. The island is referred to by the natives as "the island of the perilous passage".'

Melissa drew in her breath. 'And do we have to travel across this perilous stretch of water to get to Tanu?'

David laughed. 'Initially, yes. But after we've had our helicopter pad built the journey will be easier. We'll just pray the wind is in the right direction when we go out there. I think we'll have to rough it a bit to begin with, but not for long. This is one of the two reasons they're paying us such excellent salaries.'

'And what's the other reason?'

'Because they wanted to get medical personnel who are capable of adapting their expertise to other medical projects they're planning to finance in other unspoiled parts of the world. If we make a go of this one we'll be sent to direct other operations. The sky's the limit, my girl!'

He leaned forward and brushed her cheek with his lips. Melissa turned at the same moment, and suddenly they were kissing each other on the lips. She felt his arms moving around her, holding her in a close, comforting embrace. She dared not admit how scared she had been feeling as David had outlined the project; she was a rotten sailor, she didn't know if she would be able to 'rough it', as David had called it. But when his strong muscular arms held her she lost all her fear. She knew she would be safe so long as he was with her.

And then the feeling of safety turned to one of sensual excitement. She could feel the tingling sensations that were running down her spine as he stroked her back, his fingers caressing her with a tantalising expertise. His hard body was moulding itself against her own. She allowed him to pull her down so that she was lying on the sofa beside him, his hands gently caressing her into a feeling of utter submission. She wanted his sensual embrace to go further...she wanted to melt into his hard, muscular body until the craving she felt deep inside her was satisfied...

Suddenly he pulled away, and looked down at her with wide, tender eyes.

'Time for you to go,' he whispered softly.

Melissa felt a pang of disappointment and frustration. It would have been wonderful to stay here in David's arms. Why was he ending the passionate embrace at this crucial moment?

He ruffled her hair playfully. 'I don't want to make you do anything you might regret,' he told her.

She sat up and took a deep breath. It was going to be so difficult to come down to earth and go back to her ward! But there would be other times together, other times when she would have to decide whether to capitulate or not. . .she hoped!

The next month passed in a whirl of activity, and Melissa felt that her feet hardly touched the ground as she struggled to finish off her work on the ward and prepare for her new life out in Malaysia. She saw David briefly during their work at the hospital for the first couple of weeks, but for the final two weeks he had been called away to attend an induction course to prepare him for his new assignment. Apparently David's training was to suffice for the two of them; he would pass on all the information she needed to know, so she was beginning to feel that she would be even more dependent on him.

He was due to return to hospital on the actual day that they were to take the night flight out to Singapore. Melissa had handed over her ward the day before and was theoretically absolved of all her nursing duties. But there was one duty she had promised to perform that wasn't too onerous for her.

Her fractured femur patient, Fiona, had persuaded her to organise her wedding on the ward. Fiona's fiancé, Brian, had recovered enough from his head and chest injuries to be allowed to be wheeled to Fiona's bedside for the simple ceremony.

Simple though the ceremony was, it had taken Melissa a great deal of effort to organise. At first she had found Fiona's parents uncooperative, but after she had explained how much their daughter had set her heart on a hospital wedding, they agreed to go along with it.

And as Melissa watched the happy pair holding hands and smiling up into each other's eyes at the end of the short ceremony, she knew she had been right to pamper to her patient's wishes. Happiness always made patients get better quicker.

The hospital chaplain drew Melissa to one side and whispered, 'I must admit I was dubious about this ceremony at first, but I'm glad you persuaded me, Sister. I'm sure they'll be very happy together when they both leave hospital. When will that be?'

'A few weeks. . .or a few months—it's very difficult to say. This is why it was important for them to have the wedding now. And they're both going to be healthy and live normal lives eventually.'

Melissa broke off as she saw the ward door opening. The bride and bridegroom's relatives were crowding around her and thanking her; she made polite replies while her eyes stayed firmly on the figure by the door. David had promised to come to the wedding if he could get back from the course in time. She hadn't seen him for two weeks, and as he came striding down the ward she felt her heart fluttering dangerously. To her embarrassment, she could feel a blush stealing over her cheeks.

'Hope I'm not too late.' David stood looking down at her enquiringly.

The bride's mother moved between them, staring

up admiringly at the handsome doctor who she knew had operated on her daughter on the night of the rail disaster.

'Well, the ceremony's over, but I think you should be the one to help the happy pair cut the cake, Doctor. It would bring them good luck.'

'Yes, please do, Dr Sanderson,' called Fiona from the bed.

Fiona's uncle, acting as official photographer, organised a group photograph while the cake was being cut. Melissa, watching from the end of the bed, suddenly felt tired. There had been so much to do in these last few weeks that she wondered if she could summon the strength to get herself to the airport tonight.

Her eyes met David's as he dutifully looked up for his cake-cutting photo. Her spirits lifted as she saw him give her the briefest of winks, and she wondered if the camera had captured it.

'I'm afraid we'll have to leave you now,' David said firmly, moving across to put a hand under Melissa's elbow. 'Sister Goldsbrough and I have a plane to catch.'

'Ooh, how romantic!' exclaimed the bride's mother. 'I didn't know you two were. . .'

'Purely professional, I assure you,' David cut in. 'Goodbye, everybody.' He moved towards Fiona and patted her hand. 'Congratulations, Fiona. You deserve all the happiness you can get.' He turned to shake hands with the groom. 'Take care of yourselves.'

Melissa added her congratulations before she allowed David to guide her towards the door. His hand under her elbow was impossible to ignore. She felt a pang of sadness as she handed her keys over to the new sister.

As she and David went out through the door together the bridal party swarmed towards them, wishing them every happiness.

The doors swung to and David gave an audible sigh of relief.

'It's almost as if we were the bride and groom going away on our honeymoon,' he said laughingly.

Melissa turned her head away as she felt the blush returning.

'Hey, what did I say?' asked David with a wicked grin as he pulled her around towards him. 'Would you mind so much if it were a honeymoon rather than a medical assignment?'

'That would depend on who was the bridegroom,' she replied lightly, quickening her step.

'And who would be your ideal man?' he pursued relentlessly.

'I've never given it much thought,' she lied, wishing he would change the subject.

'But surely in your twenty-five years there must have been someone who sparked off. . .'

'And how about you?' she returned, as she stopped still in the middle of the corridor. 'You're older than me, so presumably. . .'

'I'm thirty-five. . .and yes, I've had my moments.' Suddenly David grinned. 'But I'm not going to tell all, if that's what you're hoping. . . Come on, we'll never make that plane. Are you packed?'

'Of course.'

'I'll pick you up in an hour.'

* * *

The noise of the engines drowned the supposedly soothing piped music as the plane hurtled along the runway. Melissa barely noticed the moment when they became airborne, but as she looked out of the window she could see the lights from the dolls' houses surrounding Heathrow Airport and the toy cars and buses snaking along the miniature roads. The rosy glow from the city of London lit up the night sky as the plane climbed higher, making its way towards the sea. She turned to look at David.

'It's so beautiful out there. . .like an illuminated fairyland. All the ugliness has gone, and you can only see the beautiful lights.'

He smiled gently as he reached across and put a hand over hers. 'You're going to love our tropical paradise, Melissa, and I'm going to love having you with me.'

CHAPTER FOUR

IT WAS the strangest feeling to be so close to David for hours on end! As the plane droned on through the night sky Melissa managed to calm her excitement; in fact she made a positive effort to appear cool and detached. She didn't want him to think she'd missed him too much in the two weeks he had been away. It was difficult enough coming to terms with the fact that she had longed for his return. But now that he was here, so physically close to her, she felt desperately vulnerable. . .and so totally in his power! He was her boss in more ways than one, and she wasn't sure that she could handle the situation, although he seemed to be doing his best to put her at her ease.

She watched as the pretty young Singapore Airlines stewardess in her attractive, long, side-slit skirt and tiny high-heeled shoes removed their trays. They had been served a delightful supper, and Melissa was impressed that the consortium had elected to send them out first class. It meant they had wide, fully reclining seats and impeccable service from the cabin staff. She noticed that the stewardess's beautiful dark Oriental eyelashes fluttered as she looked down at David.

'Would you like a brandy with your coffee, sir?' the young woman asked, in a soft, demure voice, with only the slightest trace of an accent.

David flashed her one of his devastating smiles, and Melissa saw the girl was instantly smitten by the handsome Englishman.

'What a good idea! Brandy for you, Melissa?'

Melissa nodded. She definitely needed something to calm her nerves. It was going to be a long night!

She sipped her brandy and pretended to watch the in-flight movie. David, she noticed, had taken out a file of papers and appeared to be studying the contents.

A tall, portly man was passing down the aisle next to David's seat. He half turned towards Melissa and she had a fleeting glimpse of a face that she thought she had seen before. But where had she seen it? It wasn't someone she knew very well.

The man moved on, and she studied the bulky frame from the back as he waited in the aisle to let one of the stewardesses go past.

Yes, that was it! she thought excitedly. He looked like Jenny's husband. But it couldn't be. It would be too much of a coincidence. Besides, she had only caught a fleeting glimpse of the man, a month ago. And what on earth would he be doing going out to Singapore? There were lots of bulky, overweight men with florid faces.

Her thoughts turned to Jenny, and she felt a pang of guilt that she hadn't contacted her again. She should have found time to give her a call, at the very least. But what could she have said? That David had convinced her she had made up the story. . .that she preferred David's version to Jenny's? And that she was going to trust David and go along with him in spite of Jenny's warning?

The thoughts tossed around inside her tired brain. It had been such a long day that she found it impossible to concentrate on anything.

Slowly she felt her eyelids drooping. The cabin lights had been dimmed and her body felt as if it were floating. She didn't expect to sleep, but she would close her eyes and rest. . .

The cabin lights flicked on and Melissa stirred in her seat. She pushed up the shutter on her window. Outside, the bright daylight made her blink. When her eyes became accustomed to the light she looked down and saw the sun shining on the sea.

'Where are we?' Without thinking, she had turned to speak to David, only to find that he was still asleep. His tousled head on the pillow reminded her so much of that dear little boy in the west London house.

She reached out and touched the dark, wavy hair, and at the feel of her fingers David opened his eyes and smiled. It was a wide, innocent smile. . .just like that of a child. . .any child, Melissa told herself swiftly. Not that particular one. No, not young Paul. He was a genetic throwback. . .wasn't he?

'I was wondering where we were,' she said softly.

He looked at his watch and then leaned across to look out of the window. She could feel the warmth of his newly awakened body, still languorous with sleep, and a sensual shiver ran down her spine.

'We're probably somewhere over the Indian Ocean, I should think.'

He leaned back in his seat, and she relaxed again. The final hours were spent having breakfast and trying to make herself look presentable for her impending arrival.

As the plane began its descent to Changi Airport, Singapore, David put his hand over hers.

'Excited?' he asked.

It was the first time he'd made any attempt to touch her in the whole of the journey, even though they had been so close.

She nodded. 'It's the first time I've ever been to the Far East. . .the longest journey I've ever made from home.'

He removed his hand and stretched back in his seat. 'Where is your home?'

Melissa gave him a dry smile. 'Where indeed? I suppose I regard England as home, but I've got no close relatives. I never knew my father; my mother died when I was very small and I was brought up by an elderly aunt who died when I was in my teens.'

She saw a flicker of surprise on David's face. Most people reacted that way. And then they were usually too embarrassed by her story to say anything else. Either that or they became overtly pitying, which she couldn't stand.

But David, being David, had to pursue the matter. 'But where do you live?'

She shrugged her shoulders. 'Wherever I work. . .that's my home.'

She expected the usual pity to flow out, but David frowned. 'Not a very satisfactory state of affairs. Everyone should have a home. . .a base where they can go when they want to lick their wounds.'

'Oh, I'm used to the situation,' she told him

blandly. 'Where do you go when you want to lick your wounds?'

His eyes veiled over for a second and then he smiled, a deep, secret smile. 'Ah, that would be telling, wouldn't it?'

'Meaning?' she enquired breezily.

'Some time, when we've got a few hours to spare, I might tell you my story.'

'That good, is it?' Melissa turned away. When people talked about their background she automatically found herself becoming brittle. She knew it was because she had suffered so much as a child from the lack of a loving family that she unconsciously felt a surge of envy towards people who had the best of everything. And she was sure that David, with his self-assured, confident attitude to life, must have been born with a silver spoon in his mouth.

She swallowed hard, as the rapid descent began to hurt her eardrums. Looking out of the window, she could see the ground rushing up to them. She held her breath...and then they were running smoothly along the runway, with barely a hint of a nudge as the pilot brought the plane to the ground.

Her first impression of Singapore after the journey through Immigration and Customs, in the relative cool of the airport air-conditioning, was that it was a giant sauna. Waiting for a taxi took only a few minutes, but she could feel the newly changed cotton blouse sticking to her skin. It was already early evening in Singapore, but the heat seemed unlikely to subside.

The air-conditioning of the taxi came as welcome relief. She looked out of the window at the intriguing sights as they were driven towards the city of Singapore. Beside the wide road she could see palm trees swaying in the evening breeze; small houses jostled beside tall skyscrapers. Some of the buildings were Chinese, some Malay, some Indian, some European.

She turned to look at David. 'What a city of contrasts!' she exclaimed.

He laughed. 'It's one of the most intriguing places on earth. But you wait until we get nearer to the centre.'

The taxi was slowing down to cope with the evening traffic. An old man pulled a trishaw bicycle alongside them and Melissa could see the effort of riding it and carrying a passenger etched on the old man's face. And then they were moving again, pulling in front of the Mandarin Hotel.

A porter took care of their luggage as they shot upwards in the lift. Melissa turned at the door of her room, but David was already moving inside his room next to hers.

'Get a good night's sleep. We've got a long day ahead of us,' he told her in an expressionless voice.

Sleep? She hadn't thought of sleep. She'd hoped they might be going out on the town.

'What time do we leave in the morning?' she asked.

'Seven,' he replied evenly. 'A boat will be waiting for us at nine on the east coast of Malaysia, and before that we have to cross the border at Johore Bahru, which can sometimes take a long time.'

There were so many questions she wanted to ask and some she dared not. For instance, why was he treating her like a distant stranger? Was he trying to reinforce the fact that he was her boss? If so, that was fine by her, but she was finding it a bit of a strain all the same after his passionate overtures of only a month ago. It was true, she had acitvely discouraged him at the time, but she hoped he hadn't taken this as a final dismissal on her part.

Swallowing hard, she wished him goodnight.

He muttered something inaudible and went into his room. As soon as the porter had gone, Melissa flung herself down on to the bed and kicked off her shoes.

Welcome to Singapore! she thought. A night in a hotel room all by myself. . .what a waste. . .and David just next door. After a few minutes she went to explore the luxurious bathroom. A half-hour soak in the large bath, pampered by the various bath oils and essences, made her feel less malevolent towards David. Any minute now he would probably phone to see if she wanted to go down to the restaurant. . .or out on the town, or. . .

She heard the slamming of David's door and waited with bated breath. But his footsteps echoed away down the corridor towards the lift. Resignedly, she picked up the phone and dialled room service.

Next morning David was already waiting down in the lobby when Melissa walked out of the lift several minutes before seven. Somehow she had managed to adjust her body clock to the new time, and had actually slept for a few hours during the night.

David directed a porter to take charge of her

luggage before asking her politely if she had slept well.

In the same distant fashion, she told him she had, and followed him dutifully out to a waiting car. The Malay driver opened her door and she climbed in. David got in at the other side and remained ensconced in his own corner, seemingly lost in his own thoughts. Oh well, if this was the way he wanted to play it, at least she didn't have to struggle with her emotions. He was only her boss, after all.

They drove through the fascinating streets, where the cultures of East and West seemed to vie with each other for supremacy. Melissa caught a glimpse of huge plate-glass shop windows displaying their wares: fabulous silks made up into Eastern and Western fashions, orchids in Chinese vases, batik shirts and sarongs, perfumes from Paris and leather shoes from Rome. She wanted to stop the car and indulge herself in an orgy of shopping, but the driver moved relentlessly on, and David sat in his corner, silently drinking in the fascinating scenes but seemingly oblivious to the fact that she was with him.

They crossed over the man-made causeway that led to Johore Bahru, the gateway to Malaysia. On either side of the causeway the deep blue waters were calm as a millpond.

They had to go through two sets of Customs and Immigration, one on the Singapore side and the other a few yards further on in Malaysia.

'They must have liked the look of us,' David said breezily, as the driver moved off along the Malaysian road after very little delay. 'We must look trustworthy.'

Melissa smiled, feeling pleased that David had actually roused himself from his seclusion. 'I don't think they go by looks,' she said, 'otherwise some of the most plausible rogues would get away with murder. I never take anyone on face value.'

'You've made that perfectly clear,' he said softly.

Oh, dear! Why had she said that? 'I didn't mean anything personal,' she began hesitantly.

He gave a dry laugh. 'Don't worry, I don't take offence easily. I've got a skin like a rhinoceros.'

Melissa decided it was best to remain silent and concentrate all her attention on the interesting scenery. They were driving along past the Sultan's beautiful palace, its fascinating white façade shining in the morning sunlight as it rose majestically out of lush, well-tended grounds.

Soon Johore Bahru was far behind them and they were bowling along an uneven road that led towards the sea. On either side the palm trees swayed in the morning breeze; they passed through a dense rubber plantation before the land opened out again as they approached the coast. Melissa could see a long sandy beach, surrounded by a few wooden houses on stilts that formed the *kampong* or village of Kota Rak.

'We've got time for breakfast,' said David, after telling the driver to wait in the car with their luggage.

The tiny Malay restaurant was actually built out over the sea. It was in deep contrast to the luxury of the Singapore hotel, but Melissa enjoyed her meal more than the lonely room service of the previous evening. The deep turquoise blue sea looked choppy as she glanced out through the open window. She turned her attention back to the Malay breakfast, trying hard not to think about the sea journey ahead.

They ate *roti*, which was a kind of Malay bread, with some *mel goreng*, fried noodles. The coffee was thick and black and too sweet for Melissa's taste—she had forgotten to specify that she didn't take sugar, not expecting it to arrive in the cup.

'Your boat is here, sir. The captain says he wants to leave with the tide.' Their driver came in through the open side of the wooden restaurant.

Melissa noticed how rough the sea was when they reached the rickety wooden landing stage. With the sun shining down out of a clear blue sky she had expected it to be as calm as the water at Johore Bahru. But a strong wind had sprung up and was whipping the waves into foam-capped hillocks that rocked the tiny fishing boat, even in the shelter of the harbour.

And then she remembered David's words. 'Is this the beginning of the perilous passage?' she asked, with an attempt at a smile.

He laughed. 'Nervous?'

'Oh, no,' she lied. 'I'm a good sailor.'

Maybe if she insisted on that she could persuade herself it was true!

And then the strangest thing happened. She thought she saw Jenny's husband again! A middle-aged, overweight man was getting out of a car that had just driven into the centre of the *kampong*. In the cloud of dust that had blown up around him she couldn't make out his features. . .but it had to be the man she had seen on the plane. Yes, of that she was quite sure.

He was paying off his driver, who was organising the luggage, and then he started to walk towards the boat.

'Wasn't that man on our plane?' she asked David.

David glanced in the man's direction and nodded nonchalantly. 'Yes. As a matter of fact we had supper together last night. Let me introduce you.'

The man had arrived at the edge of the flimsy landing stage. His heavy footsteps seemed to endanger the very construction of the jetty, and Melissa expected the whole thing to collapse into the sea before they'd even managed to board the tiny fishing boat.

David took hold of her arm, as he held out his hand to the newcomer. 'Good morning, Victor. I'd like you to meet Sister Melissa Goldsbrough, who's going to be in charge of the nursing situation on Tanu. Melissa, this is Victor Linden, one of the directors of the consortium.'

She swallowed hard as she looked up into the plump, now familiar face of what had to be Jenny's husband. There couldn't be two Victor Lindens who looked like the portly man in Jenny's driveway. The man's eyes seemed to flicker for an instant as he returned her scrutiny. Did he remember that Jenny had tried to pass her off as someone delivering catalogues?

'Haven't we met somewhere before, Sister?' he asked in a deep booming voice.

'It's possible,' she replied quietly. Quickly she turned away to look up at David. 'Shouldn't we be getting on board this contraption?'

David laughed. 'Melissa's somewhat nervous

about this journey—she's heard it can be very perilous.'

The big man gave a broad expansive smile. 'Oh, it can! That's why we're making every effort to finish off the helicopter pad. I've come out specially to see how things are going in that direction. Meanwhile we'll all have to suffer. But I agree with your description of the boat, Sister—it's certainly something of a contraption! Let me help you aboard.'

She allowed herself to be lifted into the air by this seemingly gentle giant.

'There you go, my dear,' Victor Linden said as he deposited her on the rolling deck of the fishing boat.

'Thank you, thank you very much.' And she meant it! Stepping across the awful divide between shore and boat had never been one of her favourite situations, and Victor Linden might almost have read her mind. He wasn't at all like the ogre she had imagined when she had first seen him at Jenny's. In fact she found it hard to imagine him forbidding Jenny to have her hospital friends out at the house. It was hard to imagine him forbidding anything, although he must have some sort of authority to be one of the directors of the prestigious consortium.

As she sank back against the hard wooden seat in front of the wheelhouse she found herself wondering why David and Victor had had supper together last night without her. And why were they so friendly? Jenny had said that Victor knew everything about David.

She corrected her thoughts quickly, as the surge of the ancient engines made thinking even more difficult. That was Jenny's version of the story, none of which was true, according to David. David was not the father of Jenny's child, so there was nothing for Victor to know. . .was there?

The sea beneath the boat began to swell; the waves at the sides became higher and more unpredictable as the boat left the harbour and moved out into the South China Sea.

Victor Linden was sitting on her right side and David on her left. She felt extremely safe, but desperately sick! And she had no idea how she would cope with a bout of seasickness flanked by such august personages. Should she make for the tiny cabin at the back?

No, that would only make things worse. In her limited experience she had found it was always best to stay out on deck, where the fresh air would give her a measure of comfort.

'The journey should take about two hours,' Victor told her in his loud, boardroom-addressing voice. 'But with a rough sea like this we'll be lucky to get there in four.'

Melissa swallowed hard. Four hours of this torture! Could she stand it?

David put a hand over hers. 'Are you all right, Melissa?' he enquired.

She gave a mechanical attempt at a smile. 'Yes, I'm. . .no, I'm not. If you could just reach for that bucket. . .'

David held her head at the same time as the bucket. Oh, the ignominy she felt as she leaned over and contributed her Malay breakfast!

'There, you'll feel better now,' David told her as

he deftly spirited away the contents over the side of the boat.

Melissa leaned against him gratefully, thankful that he hadn't made a fuss but simply done what had to be done. And, remarkably, she was beginning to feel better.

'You'll soon get your sea-legs,' he told her in a gentle, sympathetic voice. 'Just relax and go with the waves. Don't try to fight them. Your body will adjust itself if you let it.'

She felt his arm go round the back of her shoulders and automatically leaned against him. He felt so strong and secure. She closed her eyes and allowed herself to drift into a state of semi-conscious sleep.

'That's what the poor girl needs, a bit of shut-eye,' she heard Victor saying. The word came through to her as if in a dream., She wasn't sure if she were dreaming or waking. 'I say, David, I'm sorry Jenny turned up at your party and made a scene.'

'Oh, nobody took any notice,' David replied. 'And it wasn't your fault.'

'Well, it was, in a way. She heard me discussing it on the phone.'

Melissa kept her eyes tightly shut. She knew she wasn't dreaming now, and she had the distinct impression that David was indicating to Victor that he should keep quiet.

Gradually her pretence at sleep took on a reality and she managed to blot herself out for over an hour. When she came to, they were a long way from the coast, surrounded by mountainous waves.

She stretched herself and smiled up at David. 'I

think I might have found my sea-legs. Where are we?'

'About two hours from Tanu at the present rate of progress,' David told her, with a wry grin.

A huge wave suddenly sprayed across the bows, drenching their clothes and splashing against their faces.

Melissa looked down at her new safari shorts. She had chosen her new wardrobe very carefully in Knightsbridge, where she had been assured that she was in the latest fashion for the tropics.

'I'm glad I'm wearing my newest cruise outfit,' she told the men.

They both laughed.

'My wife is a stickler for fashion,' Victor boomed over the noise of the waves. 'Costs me a fortune, because everything changes every few weeks.'

'Victor's married to Jenny,' David put in casually.

Melissa drew in her breath but didn't reply.

'You know my wife, I believe,' said Victor.

'Yes, we were nursing colleagues before her marriage,' she told him. 'In fact, I should have been at your wedding, but I was away on holiday at the time.'

Melissa averted her eyes, thinking that Victor was either playing it very cool or he genuinely hadn't recognised her from her visit to his house last month. Well, she had to face it; she'd had difficulty recognising him, so most probably he hadn't had a good look at her that day.

'How long will you be out here on Tanu?' she asked Victor, feeling she should show some interest out of mere politeness.

'That depends on how the workmen and engineers are getting along. Not too long, I hope, because Jenny doesn't like being alone.'

'Ah, but she's got young Paul to keep her company, and help in the house. . .' Her voice trailed off. Was she giving too much away?

Victor's eyes flickered for an instant. 'Poor Jenny has suffered a great deal in recent years, so I like to be near her as much as possible. Isn't that so, David?'

David nodded, but his eyes held a veiled expression. Another huge wave deluged them, taking their minds off far-away London.

Melissa turned and clung to David as she felt the boat lurch. 'How much longer?' she whispered, feeling like a child.

His hands soothed the back of her neck and she thought she felt his lips lightly brushing the top of her head.

'There's Tanu. . .out there!'

She looked, and beyond the mist, spray and mountainous waves she could see a tiny island rising out of the sea.

'Home,' she whispered, as she snuggled against David's chest.

'Poor little orphan girl,' he murmured.

She stirred in his arms, wondering if he was mocking her, but a cursory glance at the deep brown eyes detected nothing but tenderness. She stifled a contented sigh. It was strange to feel so happy in the middle of a rough sea. There was one good thing about the perilous passage—it had brought the two of them closer together again.

And then she stiffened as she felt Victor's large hand on her arm.

'Sorry to trouble you, my dear, but I think I've got a touch of my indigestion. If you could reach down into that bag over there, I've got some of my indigestion tablets. . .oh, God!'

She turned all her attention on the obviously sick man at her side. She deduced that his pallid cheeks had nothing to do with the rolling of the boat, because he had shown himself to be a good sailor. And his sweating palms and stertorous breathing were a cause for alarm.

David was on his knees beside the sick man, reaching up to place his hands on Victor's rapidly heaving chest.

'Are you having those pains you told me about?' he demanded.

Victor nodded imperceptibly, his face an agonised mask of suffering.

David turned quickly to give Melissa his instructions, but she was already delving into the medical bag.

'Get an amyl nitrate capsule. . .you'll find some gauze. . .'

As Melissa broke open the capsule into a piece of gauze and held it to Victor's nose she knew that both she and David had come to the same preliminary diagnosis: angina pectoris. David, it seemed, had been forewarned of Victor's condition.

She felt for Victor's pulse. As she expected, it was very feeble, but the pain seemed to be subsiding, as he breathed in the fumes from the capsule.

'Hold on, old man,' David urged gently, as he pressed his stethoscope to Victor's chest.

He was frowning as he finished his examination. Turning to Melissa, he spoke rapidly in a quiet, tense voice.

'See if you can get the captain to radio ahead. We're going to need a stretcher when we pull in to land.'

CHAPTER FIVE

MELISSA could see the shoreline appearing nearer and nearer as the captain battled with the waves. She held another ampoule of amyl nitrate close to Victor's nostrils.

'It's going to be difficult to land,' whispered David, after a hurried consultation with the captain. 'Apparently they usually send out a smaller boat from the shore, but it's impossible in this rough sea, so they're going to rig up a pontoon and haul us in.'

Melissa grimaced as she turned away from their patient. 'Won't that be difficult?'

David's face was grim as he answered. 'Very.'

Victor appeared to be dozing off into a fitful sleep. Melissa moved back on to her seat at the same time as David sank down beside her.

'Had you any idea that this might happen?' she asked quietly, indicating the prostrate figure in the bottom of the boat.

David hesitated before replying, seemingly choosing his words carefully. 'He mentioned something about it last night. I must admit I was worried when I saw him lift you into the boat. But I knew he had realised he'd got angina. He's been treating himself for indigestion, like so many of these executives who can't find time to see their doctor. I was planning to examine him when we got settled in.'

'I hope I didn't cause this attack,' Melissa said concernedly.

David smiled reassuringly. 'No, no, it was on the cards. He told me he's been working long hours, taking no relaxation whatsoever and worrying about. . .all his various problems.'

'Have you known Victor long?' she asked innocently.

He gave her a wry grin. 'You're not going to worm anything out of me, my girl. . .look, they're signalling for us to start disembarking.'

'What, here? But we're nowhere near the shore!' Melissa cried in alarm.

'This is as far as the captain dares to go with the sea as rough as this. He doesn't want the boat to get dashed to pieces on the rocks.'

Melissa eyed the makeshift pontoon that was being winched out to their boat. It was made of a wooden platform lashed to some oil-drums, and it bobbed up and down ominously. A couple of wide-eyed Malay boys were sitting on it, guarding a stretcher that looked as if at any minute it could go hurtling into the water.

'Jump, *madame*!' called one of the Malays.

'Yes, go ahead, Melissa,' David urged, with a hint of a smile on his face. 'Women and children first.'

'I think I'd rather stay here,' she muttered through clenched teeth. 'I've become quite attached to this little bathtub. What about Victor?'

'One of the sailors will give me a hand,' David told her.

'Jump now, *madame*!' urged the Malay, holding out his arms.

She took a deep breath. Strong brown arms grabbed and steadied her as her feet touched the slippery pontoon. She crouched beside the stretcher, waiting for David to lower the heavy patient.

David had rigged up a fireman's sling from strong canvas and with the help of one of the sailors, Victor was lowered on to the pontoon and settled on to the stretcher.

Melissa held her breath as the pontoon groaned under the weight of too many people. Nervously she watched the men on the shore winching them in to safety. She put out a hand and took hold of the patient's. Victor's eyes remained tightly shut, but he hung on to her hand as if it were a lifeline.

He's terrified, she thought sympathetically. So was she, if the truth were known!

As the pontoon reached the shallows, several of the Malays rushed out from the shore, offering their shoulders and their arms as support to those who could wade ashore.

Melissa and David declined assistance as they waited for help with the stretcher. A couple of strong-looking young men in white orderly's uniform came running from the trees down the white sandy beach.

'That's where the main clinic is,' David explained, shielding his eyes from the sun as he pointed into the palm tree grove. 'It's the only concession to the twentieth century on this unspoiled island. We wanted to hide it away so that the rest of the island remains as it was before we came.'

Melissa could hear the pride in his voice, and for the first time she began to appreciate just how beautiful their island paradise was. Tall palm trees bent and swayed at the edge of the fine white stretch of sand that ran down to the sea. High above the beach, the rocks on top of the hill sparkled in the strong afternoon sunlight. She turned to look at David, and as their eyes met she felt a thrill of excitement running through her. She'd survived the perilous passage and they were actually here, about to start their new life together.

The orderlies had arrived and were lifting the stretcher off the pontoon. Melissa moved with them as the patient was still clinging to her hand.

'Gently, there,' David urged, as he moved alongside. 'Take it easy, boys. This is our first patient, so let's start as we mean to go on.'

'Not our first patient, sir,' one of the orderlies corrected in a shy, soft voice. 'We have some patients from the village already.'

Melissa, walking beside David, saw the frown that crossed his handsome face. 'We're not due to open the clinic until next week. Who's looking after them?' he asked.

'We are,' said one of the young orderlies, scarcely disguising the pride in his voice. 'I am qualified in first aid. Last night I delivered my first baby.'

'Did you, indeed?' David flashed a look at Melissa. 'We'd better get ourselves into the clinic as soon as possible. Heaven knows what sort of a situation we'll find!'

The clinic was a wooden, two-storey building that rose unexpectedly out of the trees. A clearing had been made in the wood, but the surrounding trees gave welcome shade. As far as possible it had been constructed to blend in with the idyllic tropical surroundings, but nevertheless, there was still a certain incongruousness about the white-painted wooden façade, the long open verandas and the closed windows of the upper floor that proclaimed they were privy to the wonders of modern air-conditioning.

David patted Victor's limp hand. 'We're here, old chap. You've done very well.'

A flicker of a smile passed over Victor's lips. 'So have you. I want to thank both of you. I'm feeling much better now, so if you'd like to set me down, I reckon I could walk from here.'

David shook his head. 'Oh, no, you don't! You're my patient now, and I'm not letting you out of here until I'm satisfied that you're a great deal better. I was going to give you a full examination, anyway. You just jumped the gun a little. Now you're going to get the full treatment.'

'Sounds ominous!' Victor quipped.

'Oh, it is. For a start, you'll have Melissa as your personal nursing sister.'

Victor gave a mock groan.

Melissa laughed, 'You're definitely on the mend!'

They settled their patient in one of the rooms on the ground floor. A Malay maid appeared with sheets and towels, hovering at Melissa's elbow and fetching everything she needed almost as soon as she thought about it.

Victor declined Melissa's offer of a light supper, saying he was tired and wanted to sleep. David gave him a sedative to ensure that he got a good night.

'I'll give you a thorough examination in the morning, old boy,' he said. Meanwhile, behave yourself. There are plenty of staff here who'll waken Melissa or me if you need us.'

Victor's eyes were already beginning to close. He gave a weak smile as he dropped off to sleep.

David stationed one of the Malay maids by his bedside with instructions to call them if the patient woke up and seemed distressed.

'Let's go and check our unofficial patients now,' David whispered.

They found half a dozen islanders in residence in one of the top rooms. The orderlies who had brought them up from the beach explained that this was the young woman who had given birth the night before and the people with her were her family. There were her grandmother and mother, who had helped with the delivery, her husband and two of her sisters.

'The grandmother wanted her granddaughter to have the benefit of hospital treatment. She was told that this is now possible, sir,' explained the young orderly, before turning to look at the oldest lady in the room. Quickly he said something in rapid Malay, and the old lady replied in the same tongue.

'I told her that you are the doctor from England, sir, and she says she would like you to examine her granddaughter and the new baby.'

Melissa saw the weariness in David's eyes as he agreed. Quietly she asked the orderlies to clear the room so that they could carry out their examination and treatment of the young mother and her baby.

It was some time before they finished. But they had satisfied themselves that mother and child were doing well, and the entire family were enjoying the luxuries of the clinic.

'I thought you might turn them away,' Melissa said softly, as they sank down into wicker chairs on the lower veranda.

'Why should I?' he replied, with a wry grin. 'They're part of the deal made by the consortium. The islanders have allowed us to use their island. It's the least we can do to look after their medical welfare.'

'Yes, but five of those people are simply hangers-on,' Melissa pointed out.

David shook his head. 'No, they're not. They're important members of the family. And they ensure that our young mother and baby get the best loving care and attention. There's more to childbirth than clinical expertise, you know. You should never underestimate the importance of the patient's nearest and dearest.'

She gave a wry smile. 'Never having had any, I suppose I'm at a disadvantage.'

He gave her a strange, enigmatic look and reached for her hand. 'I really think you should tell me about it, because I can see you've got a chip on your shoulder about it.'

'I have not!' she remonstrated, but even as she said the words she knew he had hit the nail on the head. She gave him a shy smile of resignation. 'You could be right, I suppose.'

He gave her a gentle smile but did not reply. Turning round, he gestured to one of the maids, who was sitting motionless at the other end of the veranda, obviously trying to keep cool in the early evening heat that had been building up all day.

'*Sila saya minum!*' he called.

The maid smiled and moved into the clinic, returning with a jug of mango juice and a couple of glasses.

Melissa relaxed against the cushions of her chair and took a sip of the iced fruit juice. 'I'm impressed you could order this in Malay,' she remarked.

David grinned. 'Terribly basic stuff. I only know how to ask for something to drink, so we might have been given anything. I'm so thirsty I didn't really care. But to return to the language problem—I'll lend you my phrase book. I had a crash course in basic Malay when I was away, but the teacher stressed that many of the islanders can speak some English, having picked it up from passing sailors and tourists. When the clinic staff begin to arrive next week we'll find that some of them speak Malay.'

He paused and put down his glass on a low wicker table. The sun had disappeared behind the hill and the short, long-shadowed twilight had begun.

As Melissa looked across at David, she was enjoying the wonderful stillness of the approaching night. The distant sound of the waves breaking on the shore and the wind swishing through the coconut palms made a rhythmic background for the constant drone of the insects in the bushes.

'I think I'm going to enjoy life here,' she said quietly.

David smiled. 'In your new home.'

'Don't rub it in. . .'

'Well, tell me about life as an orphan,' he broke in,

almost harshly. 'All these hints about how deprived you've been have whetted my appetite.'

Melissa took a deep breath. 'There's not much to tell. My mother married beneath her. . .or so my aunt always used to tell me. She was an only child of elderly parents and I think she wanted to get away from home. . .again, according to Aunt Dora.'

She smiled, sensing the easy rapport that had sprung up between them. She saw that David looked calm and relaxed as he listened to her story. Yes, it would be good to confide in someone at last.

'My grandfather had inherited a huge house from a distant relative; according to Dora, he struggled to keep up with the endless bills, but it was like pouring money down the drain. At one point he tried to make a go of the farm attached to the house. He was a proud man and kept up the pretence that he was one of the landed gentry. He insisted on hiring staff to do the hard work, and of course he was overextended and went bankrupt. And around the same time as this unfortunate event, my mother fell in love with one of the hired hands and ran away to Gretna Green to marry him.'

'How romantic!' said David. 'I thought you said there was nothing much to tell. I mean, did the hired hand put a ladder up against your mother's wall one moonlit night and. . .'

'Oh, come on, David, don't make fun of me,' she put in, albeit with a smile on her face. 'We're talking about my nearest and dearest, remember?'

He reached across and squeezed her hand. 'I'm sorry. . .but you must admit it is romantic, don't you?'

Melissa laughed. 'Not according to Aunt Dora. My mother, apparently, was already pregnant with me. . .'

'So your grandfather cut her off without a penny from his overdraft, did he?'

'You've got it. But this is the serious bit.' Her voice wavered slightly. She never liked to imagine her parents in their abject poverty. 'My mother was very proud, but she wasn't strong. I think she had some kind of chest complaint, but Aunt Dora was very vague. My father got a job on a farm, but when I was two months old he was killed in a tragic accident involving the farm machinery. . . I've never asked for details.'

David moved his chair nearer to hers and put his arm around her. 'Of course not. . .look, if it distresses you, don't go on.'

She swallowed. 'No, I want you to know my background.'

'If I know your background, we can put it behind us and start afresh,' he said softly.

At first, Melissa thought she had imagined the butterfly touch of his lips on her hair. . .just as she had felt on the boat. He cares for me! she thought. . .maybe more than I imagine. Underneath his flippant exterior his feelings are strong and reliable. She had to finish the story for him. . .to exorcise the ghosts of her past.

'My mother struggled on, until she was turned out of the tiny cottage that went with the farming job. She moved into a hostel, but her health was getting worse and she'd lost the will to live. When I was six months old she died. . . I think the diagnosis was bronchopneumonia, but that's no reason for a young woman to die.'

They were both silent for a while, listening to the night sounds of the island. It was David who prompted her to continue.

'And then what happened to you...after your mother died?'

'The hostel informed Aunt Dora, my grandfather's elderly spinster sister. She took me in because my grandparents had been taken into an old people's home. And every day of my childhood she told me that I mustn't grow up to be like my mother...and as for my father—well——!'

She stopped speaking and her eyes met David's. She realised that she had been unconsciously mimicking Aunt Dora's strident tones as she had finished off her story. At last she felt she could put her unhappy childhood in perspective. She remembered the gong in the hall at Aunt Dora's booming out to announce that supper was ready, and if she didn't get to the table with clean hands before the gong stopped, she was punished...and Aunt Dora seemed to relish wielding that leather strap...

She continued to stare into David's eyes, now tender with sympathy. There were some things she couldn't bring herself to tell even David. But she had told him enough to feel that she could put it behind her, try to forget and concentrate on her new life on the island which was now her home.

She leaned back against his arm, closing her eyes to savour the intimate moment.

His lips when they claimed hers sent a shiver of excitement shuddering through her body. She turned towards him, wanting to melt against his hard manly chest. His lips moved slowly from hers and she opened her eyes to see that he was holding her gently, looking tenderly into her eyes.

'Thank you for telling me your story,' he said softly. 'One day I'll tell you mine. . .but not tonight. I'm going to order us some supper, out here on the veranda, and then we're going to turn in. It's been a long day. I think we should stay here at the clinic tonight. We'll be near to Victor if he needs us. And to be honest, I couldn't face settling in to our quarters down by the sea. Tomorrow I'll take you down there.'

'You mean we're going to live down by the sea?' she asked, feeling the romantic side of her nature taking over. 'I've always wanted to sleep with the sound of waves dashing on the shore.'

He laughed. 'Tomorrow your wish shall be granted, o, Princess! I shall take you down to your wooden castle, with a thatched roof, beside the white sandy beach.'

'Mmm, sounds wonderful!' A tiny warning bell was ringing in her head. This idyllic state of affairs couldn't last.

Oh, yes, it could! she told herself firmly. The bad times were over and done with. She was in charge of her life now, and she was going to think positively about everything. . .especially David. This evening, she'd fallen head over heels in love with him, so she had to believe only the best about him. There was absolutely no truth in the rumours.

One of the maids brought their supper out on to

the veranda. They had a delicious chicken and vegetable soup, followed by fresh fruit—papaya, mangoes, pineapple and oranges. Afterwards they sat close together on the veranda, enjoying the peace and tranquillity.

Melissa's eyes had begun to close as David stood up and took hold of her arm.

'Time to turn in. We'll use a couple of rooms on the ground floor.'

She smiled; she was so tired, she could have slept on the wooden veranda floor.

They looked in briefly to check on Victor. He was still asleep; his pulse was stronger and more regular and his breathing seemed easier.

David impressed upon the maid that they must be wakened if Victor needed them, before taking Melissa off to the far end of the corridor. Facing the hillside there were two rooms, on either side.

The moon shone in through the corridor window as David took her in his arms. There was nothing passionate about the embrace, but she felt spiritually stirred. She felt there was a deep understanding between them that mustn't be shattered. At all costs, she was going to build on this feeling of mutual trust.

'Goodnight, Melissa, sleep well,' David murmured as their embrace ended.

'Goodnight,' she said softly, smiling up into his tender eyes, illuminated in the moonlight. She wanted to tell him how much she loved him, how much she trusted him. . .but a wary little voice discouraged her. Gently she moved away and opened her door. Tomorrow was another day. One step at a time. . .

CHAPTER SIX

MELISSA was awake early next morning. The sun, slanting in through the louvred windows of her ground-floor room at the clinic, was already warm on her face. She turned on her side to listen to the unfamiliar sounds, the distant sea, the droning of the insects and the swishing of the palm trees. Some children were playing in the sandy soil outside her window, and the strange unfamiliar language rose up to tease her mind.

She smiled to herself as she jumped out of bed. Today was the day David had promised to take her to her castle by the sea. He had said it was a wooden one with a thatched roof, and she deduced that it must be one of the picturesque cabins she had briefly glimpsed when they hurried towards the clinic with Victor.

As she remembered Victor she felt relieved that no one had had to waken her in the night. Obviously he must be improving, unless David had been summoned.

She showered in the small bathroom that led off from her room. Returning into her room, she quickened her step as she heard the knock at her door.

David was standing on the threshold, a towel slung casually round his broad shoulders, but otherwise his only garment was a pair of sleek, black, snug-fitting swimming trunks.

He gave her a lazy smile, and she felt her colour heightening as his eyes swept over her towel-clad figure.

'I've checked on Victor, and he's much better. So how about a swim before breakfast?'

She smiled. 'Why not? I'll just slip into my bikini.'

The domestic staff didn't seem to think it odd that their medical director and his nursing sister should wander barefoot through the clinic wrapped around in towels. Melissa smiled to herself as she hurried after David. This was the life, away from it all. What a way to start the day, compared with the hustle and bustle of London!

The white sand stretched ahead of them as they emerged from the trees. The sun, glinting on the foam-capped waves, dazzled their eyes and she had to shield them as she gazed out to sea. Another island rose out of the sea on the distant horizon, otherwise their own island dominated the land and seascape like the tropical paradise Melissa had expected.

The water was surprisingly warm as she ran into the waves, hurling herself bodily through the breakers to come out the other side where the sea was calmer. She lay on her back gazing up at the sky through half-open eyes.

'Idyllic, isn't it?'

David's voice close by startled her out of her reverie.

'Mmm,' she agreed lazily, without moving. 'I don't think I shall ever want to go back to civilisation.'

He laughed. 'Neither shall I. . .but why should

we? I said we were going to play at Robinson Crusoe.'

She joined in his laughter, turning over and running her hand through the sea so that she sprayed water on his face. It seemed so long since she had heard him telling everyone at the party that they were going to be castaways on a desert island. And she hadn't thought it could possibly be true...but it was!

David splashed water back at her in retaliation and then caught her in his arms to hold her against him in a long, lingering kiss. She allowed herself to go limp as she felt his strong arms around her. And then as her desire mounted she felt the excited, sensuous tingling of her whole body. Happily she moved in David's arms, so that his hands could caress her more and more. She leaned back on to the water, wanting the delicious sensual sensations to go on forever.

They were both laughing as they ran out of the sea and flung themselves on to a deserted cove, well hidden among the gigantic rocks and completely out of sight of the main beach. David, she knew, had deliberately steered their swimming course so that they could be alone, away from any watching eyes on the shore.

He moved on to his side and lay looking down at her on the sand. She ran a hand through her long, wet hair, feeling the soft sand mingling among the strands.

He cupped her face in his hands. 'You look like a mermaid washed up on the sand,' he said softly.

A wave tossed itself over them, and David laughed

as he leaned down to take her in his arms and carry her higher up the beach to where the sand was warm and dry.

Gently he laid her down in the sand, covering her body with his own. She could feel the strong, firm contours of his muscular frame pressing into her soft flesh. And she knew how much he wanted to make love to her.

And it felt so right that they should make love here on this sun-kissed shore of their tropical paradise. They were creatures of another world that had nothing to do with civilisation. The strong primaeval urge rising deep inside her was something she couldn't ignore, even if she wanted to. It was the most natural, most perfect idea to give herself to this man whom she loved more than anything in the world. As she felt his hands caressing her body, she leaned towards him, arching her back in delicious anticipation of her total surrender. . .

Afterwards, she lay on her back, gazing up at the blue sky that looked so much more beautiful now. In fact, the entire landscape looked as if it were part of some gigantic fairyland.

David's lips were close to hers. 'This is a good way to start the day,' he murmured.

Melissa half turned towards him. 'I didn't know this would happen,' she said softly.

He gave a dry laugh. 'I hoped it would. . . I planned it would.'

'So my seduction was on the cards, was it?' she teased him, gently. 'Was it inevitable that I would fall for your irresistible charms?'

'Oh, I've had to work on it. No one could say you

were a piece of cake...' David stopped, seemingly in mid-sentence.

'Like certain girls you could mention?' she prompted lightly.

'That's not what I was going to say at all.' He stood up and brushed the sand from his muscular limbs.

Melissa heard the warning note in his voice and remained silent. Their lovemaking had been idyllic; why spoil it by bringing up the past?

She stood up, shaking the sand out of her hair. David stood looking down at her with a quizzical expression. Suddenly he reached forward and took the sandy strands between his fingers.

'Don't try to analyse our feelings, Melissa. What we have is very special, but it can so easily be shattered. We have to live for the moment, not thinking about the past or the future. The present is all that matters. Promise me you'll believe that?'

She eyed him tentatively. 'That's your philosophy of life, but I'm a firm believer that we should live and let live, so don't try to impose your ideas on me. Of course the present is important, but we can't discount the past altogether, nor can we pretend to ignore what's to come.'

His eyes flickered dangerously. 'I hope this isn't going to cause a rift in our relationship, Melissa.'

She gave him a gentle smile. 'I hope so too.'

They began to walk back over the sand, around the rocky headland. On the main beach, a couple of fishermen were arriving with their morning catch, running their little boats high on to the sand so that they could unload.

Melissa could feel the excited springing in her step, the surge of new-found energy from her encounter with David. She loved him so much now, but at the same time she found herself feeling even more wary. He had made it quite clear that he wanted to have his cake and eat it. He believed in living for the present, so there was no point in considering a future with him. Was that what he had done with poor Jenny?

Even as the thought occurred to her she tried to dismiss it. But it lingered on just the same, through the time it took to shower and change into the white cotton dress that the maid had laid out on the bed in her room. As she stood in front of the mirror, checking her professional image, she wondered if she was simply being an ostrich, burying her head in the sand as far as David was concerned. Jenny had tried to convince her that David wasn't to be trusted. Was she merely being blind because she loved him so much?

But as soon as she saw David again she felt ashamed of her thoughts. She sat opposite him on the veranda, drinking the strong hot coffee the maid had poured out for her and watching the now familiar way that his face crinkled into a smile. A couple of baby monkeys were careering up and down the branches of the nearby trees, chattering excitedly as they swung along, seemingly oblivious to the eyes of the human beings.

'They've got so used to the islanders being kind to them that they don't have any fear of people,' David told her. 'I suppose they're living in a fools' paradise, because they could be in for a nasty shock if the wrong type of person came to the island.'

'Let's hope that never happens,' said Melissa thoughtfully, sipping her coffee. 'It would be awful if something shattered their blind trust in human nature.'

David's eyes seemed to hold hers for a long time as he replied, 'Yes, but I see no reason why that should happen. . .for the present.'

They went to see Victor after breakfast. David gave him a thorough examination before sitting down at his bedside.

'I'm going to tell you what I want you to do, Victor,' he began carefully. 'You've been pushing yourself beyond the limit for far too long. Another one of these attacks and you mightn't be quite so lucky. First of all you've got to lose some weight, and then you've got to change your lifestyle.'

Victor gave a harsh laugh. 'Easier said than done! I might be able to lose some weight, but as for changing my lifestyle. . .huh! I've got far too many fingers in too many pies.'

David leaned towards him, an earnest expression on his face. 'Exactly. . .you said it, Victor! Now ask yourself, why are you working so hard? Do you need all the money you're making?'

'No, of course I don't need all that money. But it's a good idea to add to your investments and keep on boosting your capital.'

'Even if you only live another year or so?' David asked quietly.

Victor frowned. 'Now you're being melodramatic!'

Melissa took the patient's hand firmly in her own.

'David's not exaggerating what will happen if you don't take yourself under control,' she told him. You've got to listen to him. You're in very bad shape. Besides the angina, you've got high blood-pressure and you're desperately overweight.'

Victor put up his hand. 'OK, you win! So what do you want me to do?'

David smiled. 'That's more like it! Might I suggest that you stay on here for a few weeks till we've sorted out the angina and the hypertension? I'll put you on a low-calorie diet and you can lose the weight while you're under our supervision.'

'What you're asking is impossible!'

Melissa reached forward to organise Victor's pillows as the big man hauled himself upright. 'Gently, Victor. Don't get excited,' she murmured as she saw the deep flush spreading over their patient's face.

'Why is it impossible?' David asked quietly. 'I can send a message to the consortium relieving you of your commitment to them. We can inform your secretary in London that all your business commitments for the next couple of months must be cancelled.'

'Yes, but what about Jenny?' Victor asked in an anguished voice.

David stood up and began to pace around the room. His back was towards Melissa, so she couldn't see his face when he spoke, but she could hear the ill-concealed anger in his voice.

'Jenny will survive without you. . .if survive is the right word for someone who's spoiled and pampered every day of her life. A little hardship might not be such a bad idea for the young madam.'

'Now look here, David, you've no right to insinuate that. . .'

'I'm sorry, Victor.' David swung round and returned to the patient's bedside. 'I shouldn't have said that, but sometimes I feel so angry about the whole rotten situation I get carried away. But you must see that you're not indispensable to Jenny, don't you? She's got servants to take care of her and young Paul, and she's got plenty of money. But if you continue to ruin your health, she'd have to take a drop in her standard of living.'

Victor leaned back against his pillows. 'OK, go ahead and organise it. I put myself in your hands.'

David gave a relieved smile. 'You won't regret it,' he said.

Victor gave a wry grin. 'I hope not! But before you sign me off from the consortium, perhaps you could check on the helicopter pad. If that's not nearing completion we're stymied.'

David raised his finger. 'Leave it to me, and stop worrying. I've got a vested interest in it myself. No helicopter, no medical project—it's as simple as that.'

'If you've finished with my help here, I'd like to go and see how the young mother and her baby are getting along,' Melissa put in quietly.

David smiled. 'Of course. Thanks for helping me to talk some sense into this stubborn man.'

Melissa patted Victor's hand. 'Be a good boy,' she told him.

He gave a dry laugh. 'Do I have any option?'

She was relieved to go out of the room. There had been too many undercurrents and insinuations for her liking. As she ran up the stairs to the top floor, she found herself wondering what it all meant. She remembered David's voice when he spoke about Jenny. He'd said that sometimes he felt so angry about the whole rotten situation he got carried away. What situation was he referring to? Had Victor and he come to some gentleman's agreement whereby David had renounced all rights to his son?

She paused outside the confinement-room. Paul is not David's son! she told herself. Why did she have to keep torturing herself? The rumour simply wasn't true. But if it wasn't true, what situation was it that made David so angry?

She pushed the unpleasant thoughts from her mind as she went into the room. The young Malay mother was sitting by the window, breast-feeding her tiny infant, closely attended by her mother. Melissa was relieved to see that the other members of the family had decided to go home.

She smiled as she went over to the window and sat down by the mother. The infant was suckling well; there really seemed no reason why they should stay on, but if David wanted to keep them there that was fine by her.

The baby's mother continued to hold the baby in her arms after she had finished feeding. Suddenly she looked up at Melissa and said, 'I can go home?'

'Yes, of course, if you're feeling strong enough.'

The young woman smiled and pointed to her own mother, who was hanging on her every word. 'My mother——' she began hesitantly. 'My mother is helping me.'

'Good, that's very good.' Melissa stood up. 'I'll tell

the doctor you're going home. But we'd like you to come back to see us again next week. . . OK? You understand?'

The young mother smiled. 'I come back next week. You are very kind.'

As Melissa left the room, she felt that she didn't really merit any gratitude. But perhaps next week when the clinic was officially opened she would feel that she was really beginning to earn her salary.

As she ran down the stairs, she couldn't help thinking that it was a strange situation in which she'd found herself. Here she was, being paid an exorbitant amount of money to spend her days on an idyllic island with the most exciting man she had ever met. There had to be a flaw somewhere.

Take a leaf out of David's book: think of the present, she told herself quickly. You're enjoying today. Who knows what tomorrow will bring?

CHAPTER SEVEN

DURING the week that followed there were two further births at the clinic. David and Melissa delivered both babies. At the end of the second birth, they went out on to the top veranda for some air. It was one of those hot, stifling afternoons that seemed to go on forever with no promise of a let-up in temperature. David had been forced to turn off the air-conditioning in the delivery-room because the young mother complained of being cold. She had never experienced air-conditioning before, having lived all her life on the island, and she had found the cool temperature most distressing.

Melissa leaned over the balcony and took in a gulp of warm air. She found herself longing for the relative cool of the night. 'We seem to be becoming well known as a maternity hospital,' she remarked, with a wry grin.

David laughed. 'When I was on the induction course, I was told I might experience some reservations from the islanders about using our facilities. They told me to coax them in by any means possible.'

'But I don't suppose they told you what to do if we got flooded out with patients.'

'No, they didn't. I suppose we'll just have to persuade the consortium to expand the clinic. It shouldn't be difficult. There are plenty of willing craftsmen on the island who would be pleased with the work. The helicopter pad is now fully operational ready for our first intake of patients and staff tomorrow.'

Melissa smiled, 'That's good.' She glanced across at David and saw the enigmatic look in his eyes. Was he too regretting that their solitary idyll was at an end? They had had plenty of time to themselves since arriving on the island, and no one had dictated what they should do with it, apart from the day-to-day running of the clinic. Victor had been an easy patient once he had come to terms with his new medically supervised régime; and the two births had been the easiest deliveries Melissa had ever made.

'How many patients are we expecting tomorrow?' she asked cautiously.

David shrugged. 'The final list hasn't yet been drawn up, but I was told we won't have more than we can deal with. And some of them will simply be housed in the cabins near the sea and won't require any set medical attention. They'll simply be there to recharge their batteries.'

'As we've been doing this week,' Melissa put in quietly.

David smiled and moved closer towards her, his hand lightly trailing along the rail of the balcony.

'I must admit I feel much fitter than when we first arrived,' he said. 'All this swimming and sunbathing is having a good effect on both of us. You've got quite a tan, Melissa.'

She laughed happily. It was good to feel so fit and healthy. They'd certainly made the most of the past week, swimming every day before breakfast and again in the afternoon or evening. And with her cabin being right beside the beach, she'd been able to sit out in front of it, smothered in sun-cream soaking up the sun's glorious rays.

'If you don't need me any more, I'll go back to my cabin and change into my bikini,' she told him.

'I'll come with you,' David said quickly. 'It's show-off-the-new-baby time in there, so the family won't want us hanging around. We'll come back this evening and see how they're getting on.'

As they slipped away through the front veranda of the clinic, there was an air of playing truant from school about them.

'Race you back home!' David said playfully.

Melissa started to run through the trees, feeling the welcome cooling shade on her head as she ducked under the trailing branches. It had become something of a ritual with them to race back to their cabins. And David always gave her a head start and then slowed down at the end.

'Dead heat!' David announced as they reached the front of her wooden thatched-roof cabin.

She smiled up at him. The result of the race was always the same, but it amused them, like children, just the same.

'Give me two minutes to change,' she said, as she ran up the wooden steps to her veranda and ducked inside.

She paused for a moment to look around her. It was beginning to feel like home. The hexagonal cabin, with its rough wooden walls, was all she needed in the way of comfort. The ceiling went up to a point in the middle, and a single light bulb had been fixed. There were two wooden beds that dominated half of the interior. Both had comfortable mattresses, a pillow and a couple of sheets. Blankets were entirely unnecessary in the continual heat. At the side of her bed was a wooden table on which there was a lantern and matches to be used in case of a power cut...which she had been told would be a frequent occurrence because of the unpredictable weather and the likelihood of tropical storms.

She peeled off her white cotton dress, which had become soaked with perspiration during the exertions of the day, and dropped it in the wicker laundry bin, revelling in the fact that one of the maids would remove it in the morning when she came to clean the cabin and it would be returned washed and ironed within a few hours. Mmm, she thought, it was an ideal situation, playing at Robinson Crusoe and having the luxury of a Girl Friday!

As she fastened her bikini she heard the distant drone of engines over the sea. She ran out on to her veranda and shielded her eyes against the strong rays of the sun above the water. It was then that she distinguished the whirring of a helicopter and saw the huge, bird-like contraption winging its way towards the island.

'They haven't wasted much time!' David called up to her from the edge of the shore. 'The helicopter pad was only finished yesterday.'

'But this can't be bringing the patients and staff...can it?' Melissa was aware of a sinking feeling in her stomach even as she spoke. Was this the end of the holiday?

David frowned. 'Lord, I hope not! They definitely

said they were coming tomorrow...look, just in case it's them we'd better get dressed again. First impressions count where staff and patients are concerned, and I wouldn't want to gree them in my swimming trunks.'

She moved back inside the cabin as the helicopter flew overhead. Dressed once more in a clean white uniform, she hurried outside and followed David along the beachside path that led to the clearing where the new landing strip had been constructed.

The helicopter engines had been shut off and the doors were opening as they arrived. A young Malay nurse in a white uniform looked out and waved to them. Melissa waved back. She had already decided that this was most probably the people they had been expecting to arrive the next day, so it was a good thing they looked ready for action.

The medical staff on the helicopter began helping the passengers off and David and Melissa went forward to welcome them. One of the nurses gave Melissa a pile of medical case notes, and Melissa was about to hand them over to David when she heard a familiar voice calling her name.

Her heart sank as she turned, temporarily at a loss for words, as Jenny came running over to her, her high heels looking terribly incongruous on the brand new palm-tree-framed concrete.

David had turned at the same moment, and Melissa caught a glimpse of his angry face. He had been bending over one of the patients, but now he pulled himself to his full height and advanced towards the diminutive blonde.

'What the hell do you think you're doing here, Jenny?' he shouted.

'Really, David, what a welcome! But I'll forgive you, because I know you don't mean it,' said Jenny sweetly.

'I damn well do mean it!' David snapped.

'David, please, everyone's listening,' whispered Jenny, in a plaintive tone, as she grabbed at his arm and tried to steer him over towards Melissa. 'Talk some sense into this man, will you, Melissa? Surely a girl's entitled to come and visit her husband. I've been worried sick about poor Victor ever since I got the awful news.'

'You've never been worried sick about anyone but yourself, Jenny,' David muttered through clenched teeth. 'How the hell did you get out here?'

'I got a flight to Singapore and went to stay in the consortium clinic for a couple of nights. They told me the first batch of Tanu patients and staff were due to fly out tomorrow, so I persuaded them to bring the date forward.'

David gave a sigh of exasperation. 'So we've got you to thank for this inconvenient arrival! Trust you to mess things up! And what about poor little Paul? Who's looking after him while you go gadding off halfway round the world?'

Jenny gave an unconcerned smile. 'Oh, he's quite happy with Nanny and Mrs Barnes. He doesn't need me. You really don't need to worry about him, David, because he's in very good hands.'

Melissa saw the uncustomary pallor that had spread over David's face. He cares, she thought, with a sudden realisation. He really cares about that little boy. But he hates Jenny. What has she done to make him hate her so?

'Look, David, let's leave the recriminations until later,' Melissa put in gently. 'I'm sure Jenny has come out here with the best intentions. Victor will be delighted to see her.'

David gave a dry, mirthless laugh. 'He'll be over the moon! And it's going to make his recovery so much easier.'

Jenny appeared unmoved by the sarcasm as she chattered on happily to Melissa. 'I felt it was my wifely duty to be here in Victor's hour of need. How is he?'

'He needs rest and quiet,' Melissa said firmly. 'He mustn't become over-excited or it'll bring on one of his attacks. Look, I'd rather you didn't go in to see him until we've time to take you. Let's get our patients and staff organised and then we'll see about you.'

Jenny smiled. 'Of course. No hurry. . . I'm not going anywhere. I'll just settle myself into one of those dear little cabins I saw when we flew over. I suppose I can take my pick. . .being the wife of one of the consortium directors has its advantages. . .'

'Jenny, come back here!' David called as the high heels clattered across the helicopter pad in the direction of the beachside path.

Jenny turned and waved. 'David, be a dear and bring my luggage!'

The soothing darkness of the night had fallen at last, bringing with it a certain easing of the tensions that had been mounting during the chaotic afternoon and evening. Melissa and David were seated in the large, airy dining-room that looked out over the dark, mysterious sea. This was the first time they had used this dining area, which was totally detached from the clinic, but freely accessible to all the patients and staff by a short path through the trees.

Melissa looked around the open-sided room at the people gathered there for their first meal on Tanu. She couldn't help but contrast it with the intimate suppers she and David had enjoyed on the clinic veranda or sitting under the stars outside her cabin. She wondered nostalgically if they would ever have any time to themselves again. Not if Jenny had anything to do with it!

Melissa's erstwhile colleague had stuck to her like a leech, insisting that she might be able to help. But when Melissa had called her bluff and suggested she go round the in-patients in the clinic and take the TPRs Jenny had suddenly remembered that she had to finish sorting out her cabin.

To Melissa's dismay, Jenny had moved into the empty cabin next to David. She herself was on the other side, in what she considered was the best site on the island. . .and the most romantic! She had sat on her veranda on starry evenings, with David, listening to the sound of the sea and the swishing of the palm trees, feeling that all her desert island dreams were coming true. But it wasn't going to be very romantic now, with David's ex-girlfriend only a few yards away.

As she looked across the table now at David, Melissa found herself wondering if she could suggest that Jenny move into the clinic to be near her husband. After all, that was the supposed purpose of this unwelcome visit, wasn't it? Or was there another, more hidden motive? Was Jenny still carrying a candle for David even though he was doing his best to discourage her?

'You're so lucky, working out here.' Jenny's voice at her side interrupted her thoughts. Melissa smiled. 'It has its advantages.'

Jenny grinned, her eyes on David at the head of the table. 'I can see that.' She lowered her voice to a whisper. 'You know, Melissa, I don't blame you for not taking my advice. I think I would have acted just like you. He's so irresistible. . .and I should know. . .'

'Jenny, would you pass the bread, please?' Melissa interrupted quickly. 'How was Victor when you saw him just now?'

'He was OK,' Jenny replied sulkily.

David suddenly leaned across. 'Jenny, I was wondering if you'd like to have the room next to Victor's. It's still vacant, and you'd be most useful if you were on the premises.'

Jenny appeared to think about the suggestion for a few seconds before turning it down flat. 'I think he's better off on his own. You're not short of staff, so he won't get neglected. Besides, I've fallen in love with my little cabin near the sea. Do you swim before breakfast?'

David frowned. 'Sometimes.'

A maid and one of the white-coated stewards came in carrying bowls of clam chowder. David announced that as the low-calorie diets hadn't yet been prepared for the overweight patients, the

Relax with **FOUR FREE** Romances

plus two Free gifts

Whatever the weather a Mills & Boon Romance provides an escape to relaxation and enjoyment. And as a special introductory offer we'll send you four Free Romances plus our Cuddly Teddy and a Mystery Gift when you complete and return this card. We'll also reserve you a subscription to our Reader Service which means you could go on to enjoy :

◆ **Six brand new Romances** sent direct to your door each month.

◆ **No extra charges** free postage, packing and handling.

◆ **Our free monthly newsletter** filled with competitions (with prizes like microwaves, television and free subscriptions to be won,) Special Readers' offers, Horoscopes and much more.

◆ **Helpful friendly service** from the ladies at Reader Service telephone 081-684-2141.

PLUS A FREE CUDDLY TEDDY AND SPECIAL MYSTERY GIFT.

Turn over to claim your Free Romances Free Cuddly Teddy and Mystery Gift.

NO STAMP NEEDED

Reader Service
FREEPOST
P.O. Box 236
Croydon
Surrey CR9 9EL

Send NO money now

Free Books and Gifts claim

Yes Please send me four Mills & Boon Romances, a Cuddly Teddy and Mystery Gift, absolutely FREE and without obligation. Please also reserve me a subscription to your Reader Service; which means that I can look forward to six brand new Romances for just £9.60 each month. Postage and packing are FREE along with all the benefits described overleaf. I understand that I may cancel or suspend my subscription at any time. However, if I decide not to subscribe I will write to you within 10 days. Any FREE books and gifts will remain mine to keep. I am over 18 years of age.

CuddlyTeddy   **Mystery Gift**

Mrs/Miss/Mr _____

Address _____

_____

_____ Postcode _____

Signature _____

8AIR

Offer expires 31st May 1992. The right is reserved to refuse an application and change the terms of this offer. Readers overseas and in Eire please send for details. Southern Africa write to Independent Book Services Postbag X3010 Randburg 2125. You may be mailed with offers from other reputable companies as a result of this application. If you would prefer not to share in this opportunity please tick box ☐

mps MAILING PREFERENCE SERVICE

ARE YOU A FAN OF MILLS & BOON MEDICAL ROMANCES?

IF YOU are a regular United Kingdom buyer of Mills & Boon Medical Romances you might like to tell us your opinion of the books we publish to help us in publishing the books *you* like.

Mills & Boon have a Reader Panel of Medical Romance readers. Each person on the panel receives a questionnaire every third month asking her for *her* opinion of the past twelve Medical Romances. All people who send in their replies have a chance of winning a FREE year's supply of Medical Romances.

If YOU would like to be considered for inclusion on the Panel please give us details about yourself below. We can't guarantee that everyone will be on the panel but first come will be first considered. All postage will be free. Younger readers are particularly welcome.

Year of birth .... Month ....

Age at completion of full-time education ....

Single ☐ Married ☐ Widowed ☐ Divorced ☐

If any children at home, their ages please ....

Your name (print please) ....

Address ....

....

.... Postcode ....

**THANK YOU! PLEASE TEAR OUT AND POST
NO STAMP NEEDED IN THE U.K.**

DR0891/RD

2

Do not affix Postage Stamps if posted in Gt. Britain, Channel Islands or N. Ireland

BUSINESS REPLY SERVICE
Licence No. SF195

MILLS & BOON READER PANEL
P.O. BOX 152,
SHEFFIELD S11 8TE

Postage will be paid by Mills & Boon Limited

weight loss régime would start the following day. There was a mild cheer from a couple of obviously obese men, who were looking decidedly uncomfortable in their Bermuda shorts, groaning at the seams, and huge gaudy shirts.

David had decided that there should be no special place settings. Everyone could sit where they chose. And the staff were free to come and go as their medical duties decreed. A couple of doctors had been a welcome asset to the medical team, and there were several Malay nurses to share the nursing duties, as well as an Australian nursing sister who seemed to Melissa to be extremely competent and adaptable.

Melissa had placed the Australian sister in charge of the one patient who was giving them cause for concern. The middle-aged patient who had been transferred from the consortium's Singapore clinic was recovering from a pneumonectomy which had been performed for bronchial carcinoma. David had already told Melissa that, in his opinion, the patient should have been left in Singapore for a much longer period before starting his convalescence, so they were keeping a careful watch on his condition and not taking any chances.

As soon as Melissa had finished her soup she pushed back her wicker chair and stood up. 'If you'll excuse me, I'd like to get back to the clinic and relieve Sister Watson,' she said.

David flashed her an enquiring look. 'There's really no need for you to interrupt your meal. Sister Watson is well qualified to deal with any emergency that might arise.'

Melissa gave him a polite smile. 'I'm perfectly aware of Sister Watson's qualifications, Dr Sanderson.' Oh, how formal it sounded to be giving David his full title again, she thought, as she walked across to the veranda and went down the steps to the path that led to the clinic.

As she walked on between the moonlit trees, she knew that if the truth were known she couldn't stand sitting next to Jenny a moment longer! She had changed so much since she had been a friendly, helpful hospital colleague. What was it that had made her like this? It was almost as if she was putting on an act. And why on earth had the wretched woman decided to come out and spoil their tropical paradise?

'It's so annoying!' Melissa told a tall palm tree, as she stood stock still in the middle of the path. She and David had been so idyllically happy until Jenny came to remind them of the past. But what was in that past? Was it as bad as Jenny would like her to think?

'What's the matter, Melissa?'

She turned guiltily at the sound of David's voice. He was standing near to her, his increased breathing indicating that he had hurried after her.

'I'm concerned about the new patient,' she said quickly. 'I don't think we're equipped to cope with the complications of a pneumonectomy if they should occur. I don't know why he insisted on coming out here so soon after his operation.'

David put a hand under her chin and gently raised her face to look at him. 'The reason he wanted to come here so soon was that he's just been given a new lease of life. This time last month, he thought he was going to die. So he wants to make the most of every precious minute of his life. I can understand how he feels, even if I don't think his doctors were wise to allow him to come here.'

He paused, still cupping her chin in his hands, his dark brown eyes probing deep inside her.

'But that's only one of your worries, isn't it?' he pursued relentlessly. 'In the few short days we've had together, I've come to understand you, Melissa, probably almost as well as you understand yourself. . .and I can see that something is wrong. You've got to confide in me. Is it Jenny?'

She drew in her breath, her eyes flickering dangerously as she stared up at him. There was no need for her to answer. He understood well enough.

'You don't trust me, do you?' he said softly. 'You believe there was something between us, don't you?'

She wrenched herself away from his grasp. 'I don't know what to think any more. I'm so confused by the whole situation.'

'But you promised to trust me,' he reminded her gently. 'It's unfortunate that Jenny has turned up just when. . .when we were getting to know each other so well.'

'Getting to know each other!' Melissa echoed, her voice dangerously calm and quiet. She had given herself to this man so completely during the past few days. She had trusted him implicity, thrown caution to the wind, surrendered all her inherent inhibitions.

She took a step backward. 'I trusted you, David, you know that. But when the past turns up to confront us like this, it's difficult not to have doubts. You told Victor it was a rotten situation that made you angry...'

She broke off as she saw the hurt look on his face.

'I shouldn't have said that,' David whispered in a barely audible voice. 'I wish you hadn't reminded me.'

Melissa took a deep breath, knowing that she had him at a disadvantage. 'But what was there between you and Jenny?' she persisted.

'Nothing!' David's eyes blazed angrily as he faced her on the moonlit path. 'Jenny chased me, and when I told her she wasn't my type, she started to make up stories about me. You know the old saying: hell hath no fury like a woman scorned. That's all there was to it.'

He broke off at the sound of footsteps on the path from the dining-room. Jenny's face in the moonlight looked decidedly smug and self-satisfied.

She moved up to David and put her tiny hand, with its long, well-manicured nails, on his arm.

'You're not a very convincing liar, my love,' she said softly.

CHAPTER EIGHT

THE loud, insistent clanging of the clinic emergency bell broke through the silence of the tropical night. Melissa experienced a powerful surge of adrenalin running through her. Only seconds before, Jenny had made her damning condemnation of David, and Melissa had been reeling from the impact of those unwelcome words. Was David really lying when he said there had been nothing between himself and Jenny?

Melissa knew there would be no time to find out at the moment. David was already sprinting through the trees towards the clinic. She had caught a glimpse of his distressed, ashen face when Jenny had made her latest accusation. How he must have welcomed the interruption that occurred immediately afterwards! It had certainly got him off the hook. . .but not for long! Oh no; Melissa vowed she wouldn't let him duck the issue this time.

Her feet moved automatically towards the clinic. Jenny was close behind her.

'Can I help?' she asked Melissa, in a breathless voice.

'I don't know until we find out what's happened,' Melissa replied in a terse voice. 'Go in and stay with Victor. Try to keep him calm. The loud bell may have distressed him.'

Melissa headed for the top floor where their pneumonectomy patient was being nursed. It was her guess that Sister Watson had some kind of emergency on her hands.

David had left the door to their patient's room open as he had run inside, only seconds before her. The young Australian sister was leaning over the patient, trying to ease the coughing attack.

'Let's get him lying on his operated side, with the good side uppermost,' David said in a calm voice. 'That way the secretions from the dead space won't flood the good bronchus.'

Melissa tried to soothe the patient as the three of them turned him on to his side. She glanced at the fluids secreted during the coughing fit, noting that there was too much serum-stained brown fluid, which indicated that there was changed blood.

David was looking at her now across the patient, his eyes deadly serious. He's made the same diagnosis as I have, she thought: broncho-pleural fistula. It was a relatively rare post-operative condition nowadays, but she had nursed a patient with it during her hospital training.

'We'll have to aspirate the fluid,' David told her quietly. 'I'll set up the machine, if you'll take over here. Sister Watson, bring some morphine.'

Melissa smiled reassuringly at the patient. The notes were spread out on his bedside table: Geoffrey Collier, age forty-two.

'Just try to relax, Mr Collier, you're in good hands,' she said gently. Dr Sanderson is going to get rid of some of the fluid that's irritating your chest. I'll give you a shot of morphine to ease the pain.'

'It's gone wrong, hasn't it?' the patient whispered. 'I should never have come out so soon. But I really thought it would do me good to get away.'

David patted the patient's hand. 'I think we may have to take you back to Singapore for a while. The surgeon will have to check what's going on.'

'You mean open me up again?' Geoffrey Collier whispered.

'Well, that would be the most sensible thing to do,' David replied. 'So we'll try to take you back by helicopter tomorrow. Meanwhile, I'm going to try to deal with the pain in your chest.'

Melissa spent the next few hours beside the patient's bedside, constantly checking on his condition. As soon as the work eased, she sent Sister Watson off to get some sleep. David had already intimated that the Australian sister would be in charge of the nursing staff the next day. He hadn't yet said what he was expecting Melissa to do, but she had a pretty shrewd idea. He had made it quite plain that he was going to accompany the patient to Singapore, and he had gone off to the newly installed telephone to make the necessary arrangements.

Melissa tried hard to stay awake, but as the night wore on she dozed off in the bedside chair. Some time during the early hours of the morning, she came to with a start as she heard the patient muttering in his sleep. Leaning across, she checked on the aspiration machine. Fluid was still being aspirated from the chest cavity. She was relieved to find that Geoffrey Collier had fallen into a deep sleep and didn't seem to be in any pain.

Suddenly her sharp ears detected the barely audible sound of muffled voices in the corridor. Maybe it was a couple of maids whispering out there. She was dying for a cup of tea! Perhaps she could persuade one of them to bring one up.

She tiptoed noiselessly to the door and opened it ajar. As she peeped out into the corridor, her heart sank. Several yards along, standing in the moonlight by the window, she could see David, his hands resting on Jenny's shoulders.

His subdued voice was barely discernible. 'We can't live in the past,' he was whispering. 'Let it be, Jenny.'

Melissa froze as she saw him bend his head and gently kiss Jenny's forehead.

Noiselessly she closed the door and leaned against it, her breathing rapid and shallow as she tried to make sense of the intimate scene. She opened her eyes wide and stared around the patient's dimly lit room. Perhaps she was dreaming. She felt pretty groggy.

She moved back to the chair and settled herself in again, longing for the morning as she stared, wide-eyed, out through the window at the night sky.

When David came in to check on the patient it was already daylight.

'I think we can disconnect this machine now,' he told Melissa. 'But we may have to connect it up again when we get to Singapore.'

'When we get to Singapore?' she repeated, in a dazed voice.

David smiled. 'Look, I'm sorry you haven't had

much rest, but you're the obvious choice. I need a competent nursing sister with me. Mike Brent, our new Australian doctor, can take my place here and Shirley Watson can fill in for you. We'll only be away for a couple of days—just long enough to settle our patient into hospital. I rang NUH—that's the National University Hospital in Singapore—last night, and the surgeon who operates at the consortium clinic has agreed to investigate our little problem here.'

The patient suddenly put out his hand and touched Melissa's arm. 'Will they let me come back to the island afterwards?' he whispered.

Melissa smiled. 'I expect so, if you behave yourself this time. Don't rush things. You can't hurry the body. It will heal in its own good time.'

She turned to look at David. 'When do we leave?' she asked.

'In about an hour. The helicopter's on standby for us.'

'You could always take Jenny with you,' she remarked casually. 'She's a trained, experienced ex-sister.'

David frowned. 'No, definitely not. Beside, I need her to stay here and keep Victor on his régime.'

'Ah, so her coming out here hasn't been a total fiasco,' Melissa said evenly.

David's eyes narrowed. 'I'm sure I don't know what you're insinuating. I know Jenny started making her false. . .'

He broke off, glancing down at the patient. Firmly he took Melissa by the arm and propelled her over to the window.

'Can't we have a truce?' he said. 'This has gone on long enough.'

'I agree, it's gone on too long. The situation, as you said yourself, is unpleasant. Yes, by all means let's have a truce,' she told him in a cool, professional voice.

He looked unconvinced. 'Fine, I'll send Sister Watson to relieve you. Be ready in an hour.'

Melissa went back to her cabin as soon as Shirley Watson relieved her and packed an overnight bag. There would be time for a quick shower if she hurried. The simple but clean and functional shower-room was situated down a couple of stone steps at the back of her room. It always felt cooler than the rest of the little cabin, as the sun never reached it.

She felt refreshed as she climbed back into her little room and sat down on the bed to brush out the tangled strands of hair. As she raised the brush to her head she heard footsteps on her veranda, and her pulse quickened as she tightened the towel around her. Perhaps David was coming to invite her for a swim. Maybe he'd delayed the departure of the helicopter.

But her heart sank as Jenny appeared in the open doorway, her face smiling happily, as if she hadn't a care in the world.

'Mind if I come in?' she asked breezily.

'I haven't much time,' Melissa replied tersely, as she continued to disentangle her hair.

Jenny moved towards her and sat down on the other bed, seemingly unaware of her cool reception. 'I know you haven't much time—David told me. He's asked me to stay and look after Victor, so of course I agreed.' She gave a simpering giggle. 'I could never refuse him anything!'

Melissa put down the hairbrush, feeling she would like to throw it at her erstwhile friend! 'Jenny, come to the point,' she said shortly. 'What's all this about? David has made it perfectly clear that he's not interested in you. . .that you're only here on sufferance. . .'

Even as she said the words, she had a mental picture of David and Jenny standing in the moonlit corridor of the clinic.

Jenny smiled confidently and stood up. 'Don't be put off by what David says. He's putting on an act so that Victor won't be jealous. Very convincing, isn't it?'

She moved to the door and stood motionless on the threshold, a mocking smile on her lips as she looked at Melissa.

'Don't say I didn't warn you, Melissa.'

The helicopter rose above the sea. From her vantage point by the window Melissa looked down at the foam-flecked waves shining in the morning sunlight. There had been no time for a swim that morning. . .not for her, anyway. She found herself wondering if Jenny and David had swum earlier.

She looked across at where David was busily checking on their patient's condition. He looked calm and relaxed, in his cool white cotton drill pants and open-necked shirt. She could see the dark hairs on his chest and wondered if he'd plunged into the sea that morning in his body-hugging black trunks.

He seemed to sense her scrutiny, because he

looked up from the patient and smiled. She was relieved that he couldn't read her uncharitable thoughts! As she smiled back, she told herself she would make a big effort not to spoil their time together. She'd got him all to herself. . .well, give or take a few doctors, nurses and patients! But at least she wouldn't have the physical shadow of Jenny hanging over her all the time.

They touched down at Selatar, the small military airport on the outskirts of Singapore, and an ambulance rushed them to the National University Hospital.

Melissa was impressed by the high-tech appearance of the hospital and the efficiency of the staff. In less than an hour they had settled in their patient and had a discussion with the surgeon who would perform the emergency operation that morning.

The surgeon explained that he would have to reopen the chest to repair the fistula. He suggested that they telephone him during the afternoon, so that he could report the patient's progress.

As they walked out of the air-conditioned hospital the true temperature of the day hit them.

David took hold of Melissa's hand and hurried her across the road. 'Let's get a taxi and explore this wonderful city,' he said. 'There's no point hanging about here. Our patient's in good hands.'

She smiled, feeling some of her earlier tension disappearing. 'How long do we have here?' she asked.

'We go back tomorrow with a new intake of patients from the consortium clinic. We've got hotel reservations, so let's go and settle in. Then we'll go out on the town.'

They checked into the Mandarin again. As the lift went upwards to their rooms, Melissa found herself thinking that it seemed like a lifetime since she'd been here before instead of just over a week. So much had happened in their relationship!

'Give me a few minutes to change into something cooler,' she said, as she paused outside her door.

'Don't take too long,' David said gently. 'We mustn't waste a minute of our precious time here.'

She heard the tenderness in his voice and marvelled that he could so quickly turn on the charm again with her. But she told herself that she had to trust him again...if only for today!

'It will have to be a whistle-stop tour,' he told her, his eyes gleaming with excitement, as they climbed into a taxi. 'What would you like to see first?'

Melissa hesitated before answering. 'The shops...some of those fantastic shops we saw when we were here before we went out to Tanu.'

The taxi whisked them away to Orchard Road. David pretended to be interested as Melissa rushed from store to store, buying perfume, a couple of silk scarves and a batik shirt that would go well with the shorts she had bought in Knightsbridge. She realised she was in danger of spending all day in the shops, so she deferred to David's suggestion that they should see something of the older part of Singapore.

Back in a taxi, they moved rapidly through the traffic along past the Istana, or President's Palace, residence of the Governor-General of Singapore during the colonial period.

'We're making for one of the older parts of the city,' David told her as the streets became narrower. 'This is known as Little India.'

They got out of the taxi in Serangoon Road and wandered along the narrow streets, past shop-houses and stalls where the exotic colours of sarees and flower garlands shimmered in the midday sunlight.

The distinctive aroma of herbs and spices floating out through the doorway of an Indian restaurant reminded Melissa that she was hungry. The thought must have occurred to David at the same moment, because he turned to look at her enquiringly.

'Do you like curry?' he asked, smiling down at her.

'Love it!' she answered enthusiastically.

'Then this is the place. One of the best curries in the world here.'

'Banana Leaf Restaurant,' she read from the sign over the door.

David took hold of her arm and ushered her inside. A smiling waiter came to welcome them, leading them to a table and placing huge banana leaves in front of them.

Melissa laughed, 'Now I see where the place gets its name!'

David smiled. 'These are our plates,' he told her. 'Curry tastes fantastic off banana leaves. At the end of the meal, they simply throw them away.'

'What a brilliant idea. . .no washing up! It's an idea that could definitely catch on.'

She was feeling more relaxed as she faced David

across the table. The tension of the night was fast disappearing, and Jenny and her awful insinuations didn't exist.

They pooled their ideas on what to order from the menu and finished up with far too many side-dishes. The smiling Indian who owned the restaurant brought a jug of foaming beer to the table and poured it out into huge glasses that resembled beer-steins.

Their eyes met as they raised their glasses over the delicious food.

'Cheers!' Melissa's eyes were dancing with happiness as she put the glass back ont he table. 'I can't help feeling a pang of anxiety about our poor patient stretched out on the operating table.'

'He's in good hands. . .one of the finest chest surgeons I know. Melissa, you've got to realise that worrying about things you can't change is a useless occupation. I'll ring the hospital this afternoon. But for the moment, let's enjoy ourselves.'

She smiled in response, wishing she could have such a basic philosophy of life as David had. He was quite right: it was futile to worry.

The food from her banana leaf tasted delicious. She tried to sample as many of the exotic side-dishes as she could, which all added to the enjoyment of her delicately spiced chicken.

After lunch they hailed another taxi and went into what David said was the heart of the old colonial Singapore. They passed Raffles Place and the bustling waterfront and drove on to Chinatown.

After exploring the narrow streets of Chinatown on foot, drinking in the authentic sights, smells and sounds of the old and new Chinese community, Melissa began to feel her energy flagging.

'We've time to have a quick look at the Botanic Gardens,' David told her, when she confessed that she was tired. 'You must see the fantastic orchids. . .the best in the world!'

She found his enthusiasm infectious as they climbed once more into a taxi. Alighting at the main gates of the Gardens, they walked up the broad sweep of the path and made their way to the orchid garden. It was a beautiful walk before reaching the orchids, and Melissa forgot how tired she was as she drank in the view of the lake, with its terrapins and exotic birds, and the fabulous tropical plants and trees.

The orchid garden took her breath away, and she turned to look up at David. 'It's like a dream, being here. . .'

He squeezed her hand. 'I knew you'd love this place. . .but I mustn't tire you. You must go back and rest now before we go out again this evening.'

They telephoned the hospital from the hotel lobby and were able to speak to the surgeon. As they had suspected, there had been a broncho-pleural fistula. The surgeon had reopened the chest and repaired it satisfactorily. He assured them that their patient was responding well to treatment.

'If all goes well I'll send him out to you for convalescence,' he told David.

'That's good,' David replied. 'But not too soon. Transfer him to our Singapore clinic before he comes out to Tanu so that we can assess his condition.'

Melissa flung herself down on the bed as soon as

she had closed the door to her room. She kicked off her shoes, turned on her side and closed her eyes. If she was going out on the town with David she wanted to look her best!

CHAPTER NINE

MELISSA was still lying on top of the bed when she awoke in her hotel room, but she felt refreshed by the couple of hours' sleep. Outside she could see that the sky was already dark, but it held a luminous glow from the many city lights.

With a sense of rising excitement she showered, before pulling out the contents of her overnight bag. There wasn't much to choose from! Perhaps she'd look best in the black and white cotton catsuit with the only pair of decent sandals she'd brought. Somehow her heart hadn't been into packing much glamour this morning. She wished she had given it more thought.

She was fixing the silver earrings she had bought for herself with her first decent salary cheque when there was a tapping at the door.

David looked cool and casual in a navy blue blazer and light grey slacks.

'You look nice,' he told her, his eyes skimming over her slender figure. 'But don't put your hair up.' Gently he uncoiled it and spread it over her shoulders. 'That's much more romantic.'

The touch of his fingers unnerved her more than she cared to admit. 'Where are we going?' she asked quickly.

He smiled. 'Wait and see. I'm taking you to one of my favourite restaurants. I think you'll love it.'

* * *

They got out of the taxi and walked a few yards along a path that was set well back from the road. Suddenly the path diverged into a garden where an illuminated fountain was playing in the middle of a courtyard. There were tables outside, set amid the exotic, scented frangipani and bougainvillaea.

Melissa smiled as the waiter showed them to a table under the stars. 'It's difficult to believe we're in the heart of a great city. Is this typical of Singapore restaurants?'

David laughed, leaning across the table to put his hand over her own. 'Nothing is ever typical of Singapore, because there are so many cultures here. It's completely cosmopolitan. The owner of this restaurant, for instance, is French.'

The waiter brought them champagne in an ice bucket and they clinked their glasses together over the starched white tablecloth. When Melissa took her first sip she saw David's eyes held nothing but tenderness for her, and she felt renewed faith in him.

David ordered oysters and Melissa chose fresh asparagus to start with. Then they both had *gigot d'agneau en croûte*—a delicious leg of lamb in pastry—served with lightly cooked spinach and duchesse potatoes.

Melissa noticed that as it was a French restaurant, the cheese was served next, followed by her choice of dessert, which was fresh strawberries.

During the meal, their conversation had been deliberately light and impersonal. It was as if neither of them wanted to break the special rapport that was building up between them. Melissa leaned back in her chair as her eyes strayed around the tiny garden of the restaurant. From the lighted interior she could hear the sounds of someone playing a saxophone. Looking through the wide open doorway, she saw that the saxophone player had attracted a crowd of young people around him.

The music stopped and the crowd cheered, clapped their hands and stamped their feet.

'I don't know much about this kind of music,' Melissa remarked, 'but the musician certainly seems talented. At least, his fans seem to think so.'

David smiled. 'I'll introduce you when he's finished.'

Melissa laughed, 'You seem to know everyone.'

He shrugged. 'Not everyone. . .but I should know this young man. He's my brother.'

She stared at him, her eyes wide with surprise. 'You didn't tell me you had a brother. . .and especially one who's out here.'

His eyes remained steady. 'That's why I brought us here tonight. I want to meet him again. It's a long time since we saw each other and I heard he was in Singapore.'

She heard the calm, no-nonsense, touch-me-not tone of David's voice. He's a dark horse, she thought. Bringing me out, wining and dining me. . .and all so that he can meet his long-lost brother!

Her eyes strayed back to the enthusiastic group inside the restaurant and in particular to the man on the small stage, who seemed to be putting all his heart and soul into the poignant slow number he was playing. She would never have guessed that this was David's brother. His face was almost concealed beneath a long, dark, shaggy beard, but she could see that he was sporting a deep, weather-beaten suntan.

His clothes looked clean but crumpled: torn, faded blue jeans, that were more patches than original material, worn with a red and black shirt, open down the front to reveal a dark hairy chest. . .that bit looked like David! But that was the only family likeness as far as she could detect from where they were sitting. And she knew that the musician was completely unaware of her scrutiny from the darkened garden.

The music came to an end some time after midnight. Melissa sensed that David was getting nervous. Twice he half rose from his chair when he thought his brother was about to leave the restaurant.

'I missed him last time I was here,' he muttered, through clenched teeth. 'I don't want the same thing to happen again tonight.'

Melissa's eyes narrowed. 'When were you last here?' she queried.

David gave a wry grin. 'The night we arrived from London. This was where I met up with Victor.'

She frowned. 'Tell me, why was I excluded from that particular little supper?'

He hesitated. 'I'd rather not say. . .look, Mark's coming out through the door. Stay here, Melissa!'

David had bounded to his feet and was hurrying past the fountain, heading towards the restaurant door. Melissa held her breath as she saw the two men meeting face to face at the edge of the garden.

The light wasn't strong enough to discern what was really happening. She longed to run after David and witness the reunion for herself, but from force of habit she obeyed her boss and remained in her seat.

The two men were looking at each other. She saw the man who was David's brother take a step backwards as if to evade the confrontation, but then David had reached forward and taken the man by the shoulders. They were much of a height, both very tall and of an athletic build. Yes, she could see the family resemblance now. But that awful unkempt beard and the shabby clothes. . .

They were coming over. David had obviously persuaded his brother to join them. Melissa felt butterflies dancing in the pit of her stomach as she watched the two men nearing the table.

David arrived first, his eyes shining excitedly. 'Melissa, I'd like you to meet my brother Mark.'

The other man was holding back, standing behind David, obviously an unwilling participant in the reunion.

'Mark, this is Melissa,' said David, urging his brother to come forward.

It was then that Melissa realised that the man was much younger than she had thought. The dark eyes above the grubby beard held a vulnerable, almost childlike expression, and beneath the ill-fitting clothes David's brother was painfully thin.

She stood up and moved towards the young man. 'Hello, Mark. I enjoyed your music.'

The young man's reaction was swift. 'Don't patronise me!'

'Mark, don't be so rude!' David said quickly.

'It's OK,' Melissa put in quietly. She turned to look at David's brother and again discerned the sensitive look in his eyes. He's been hurt, she thought. But who hurt him? And why this rift between the two brothers? 'Why don't you come and sit down with us?' she suggested. 'Would you like a drink?'

The young man shrugged. 'OK. I'll have a Coke.'

Melissa breathed a sigh of relief as David's brother sat down on the chair next to her and sprawled his long legs under the table. David signalled for the waiter.

'I think this calls for more champagne,' he said.

'Do we have something to celebrate?' Mark asked in a cool deliberate tone.

David reached across and put his hand over his brother's. 'You know we do. I've been trying to find you for ages. This was one of the reasons I took on my latest medical assignment, because it meant I could come out to the Far East. I knew you were out here somewhere. How are you managing to survive?'

The young man shrugged. 'I make a living...enough to eat. I take any job that comes along. This one is great. I play two or three times a week, filling in for the resident guy who's off sick. He's coming back tomorrow...so you only just caught me, because I'll be moving on.'

'Where to?' David asked anxiously.

His brother shrugged. 'Haven't decided yet. Wherever the spirit moves me.'

'Come back to Tanu with Melissa and me! We

could do with an extra pair of hands.' David turned to Melissa. 'Mark was a medical student, but. . .'

'Oh, no! You're not going to get me on that again. When I dropped out of medical school it was for good!'

'You're terribly thin,' Melissa said quietly. 'The food's good out there. Why don't you come and let the staff pamper you? We specialise in slimming diets, but I'm sure they could concoct the reverse idea. You know, dressed like that, you remind me of a scarecrow! What you need is a bit of flesh on your bones. . . I'm speaking purely from an objective medical point of view, you understand. It doesn't matter to me what you do with your life. May I have some more champagne, David?'

As she held out her glass, she found her hand was in danger of trembling. Beneath her cool exterior she was scared of David's antagonistic brother!

The three of them were silent as David poured out the champagne into Melissa's glass. It was so quiet she could hear the bubbles effervescing to the surface.

'I suppose you think you can kill the fatted calf and the prodigal will come running back,' said Mark, after several seconds had elapsed.

'Please don't do us any favours!' Melissa declared as she took another sip of her champagne. 'Shouldn't we be going back to our hotel, David?'

There was a ghost of a smile on David's lips as he nodded. 'It's been nice meeting you again, Mark, but we must go. Got a busy day ahead of us tomorrow.'

'OK, then tell me something,' the young man said.

'If I did decide to come out to this island of yours, how would I get there?'

'Come round to the Mandarin Hotel in the morning. We might be able to squeeze you into the helicopter. . .' David began.

His brother shook his head. 'Too soon. I need time to think.'

David frowned. 'Well, if you're coming under your own steam, you'll have to take a fishing boat from Kota Rak on the east coast of Malaysia.'

'Food's good, is it?' Mark turned to look at Melissa.

She smiled. 'Not as haute cuisine as this restaurant, but pretty good all the same.'

The young man pulled himself to his feet, a pensive expression on his face. 'You might see me. . .and then again, if I get a better offer, who knows? Goodbye.'

Melissa hardly dared to look at David's face as he watched his brother walking away through the restaurant garden. It was only when she felt his hand stealing over to her own that she turned her head and their eyes met.

'What happened, David?' she asked gently. 'How does a young man become embittered like that?'

David shook his head. 'It's a long story. Some time I'll tell you all about it. . .but not now.'

Melissa gave a wry smile. 'You keep promising to reveal the skeletons in your family cupboard. I'm beginning to think you've got something you want to hide!'

David's face suddenly cleared and his firm confident manner returned. 'Come on, Cinders, let's get you away from here before your carriage turns back into a pumpkin!'

As their taxi wended its way through the Singapore streets, Melissa had the impression that she was in a city that never slept. People were still walking along the side of the roads, cars were coming at them from all sides, and restaurant lights continued to shine invitingly from wide, flower-bedecked windows.

She noticed that David was uncharacteristically quiet and subdued. It was as if the meeting with his brother had cast a shadow over their evening.

Neither of them spoke as they went up in the hotel lift to their rooms. Melissa fished her key from her bag and turned to say goodnight to David.

His dark eyes, looking down at her, were sensitive, making him look almost as vulnerable as his young brother. He reached for her key and opened the door.

'May I come in?' he asked, in a gentl voice.

Melissa's heart started to thump madly as she gave him a nervous smile. 'Would you like a nightcap?' she asked.

He shook his head. 'No. . . I want to talk.'

At last! she thought hopefully. Maybe she could get some answers to her questions.

He closed the door and reached out for her. As he held her in his arms, she sensed the sadness and disappointment that he was experiencing.

'Were you ever close to your brother?' she asked gently.

He nodded, holding her shoulders as he looked down at her in the subdued lighting of the bedroom.

She saw that the maid had been in to turn down the huge king-size bed, and the curtains had been pulled, giving a cosy, country-house atmosphere.

'We were very close before he left medical school. . .but he's changed so much.'

David took her hand and led her over to the window, drawing back the curtains so that they could go out on to the balcony. They stood together, leaning against the rail, listening to the subdued sound of the night-time traffic far below them.

'I was his father-figure, you see,' David continued pensively. 'He's ten years younger than I am, and he never knew our father. Our parents were killed in a car crash when he was just a few months old. Mark and I were on the back seat. . . I remember he was in his carry-cot and he started to cry. The front of the car was all crumpled up where the lorry had hit us, but I wondered why my parents were keeping so still. Then someone smashed the rear window. . .there was glass everywhere. . .and pulled Mark and me out. You know, I remember it as if it were only yesterday. Ten-year-olds have remarkable memories, I suppose.'

David's hand was still holding Melissa's and she felt the tension of his fingers as he reminisced.

'I'm sorry—so sorry,' she murmured gently, feeling the inadequacy of her sentiments.

'Oh, it was all a long time ago. But that was why Mark and I were so close. They put us in a children's home because our grandparents said they couldn't cope with us. Every time they tried to separate us I insisted we stay together. When I got my scholarship to medical school, Mark came with me. I was nineteen and he was only nine. I rented a room near the hospital. I used to take him to school in the mornings every day until he was eleven. Then he became more independent, but it was inevitable that he chose medicine as a career.'

Melissa drew in her breath. 'But why did he drop out of medical school.'

'He got involved with a girl. . .one of those unfortunate affairs that can change a young man dramatically. She jilted him and broke his heart. I think that had been the first female love he'd ever known. In effect, the girl had been mother, sister and girlfriend to him, and he couldn't handle the rejection. . .so he dropped out. He's been living rough ever since. Last year one of his old school pals told me he'd seen him in Thailand—apparently Mark was travelling around in the Far East. I made extensive enquiries and found that Singapore was one of his favourite destinations.'

'But why did he want to cut himself off from you?' Melissa asked gently. 'I would have thought you could have consoled him.'

She looked up enquiringly and saw the hurt look in David's eyes. He waited a few seconds as if searching for the right words.

'He blames me for the split with his girlfriend. He thinks. . .oh, it's all so complicated!'

'Don't talk about it if it distresses you,' she put in hurriedly.

He gave her a tender smile. 'You're so understanding, Melissa. Tonight I was so grateful for the way you handled Mark. It was almost as if you'd known him all your life.'

She smiled up at him. 'He's very like you. . .and I've had to learn how to handle you.'

She saw the tender, enigmatic expression in David's eyes and her pulses raced. His mouth hovered sensuously above her, the lips parting to display his strong white teeth. And then he was kissing her, at first gently and then with a fierce passion that roused all her senses.

She felt his arms reaching around her to lock her in his firm embrace. Their bodies moulded together as he caressed her skin, evoking a rapturous response from deep inside her.

And then he was lifting her up, carrying her over to the wide, sumptuous bed. She gave a sensuous sigh as he lay down beside her, pulling her once more into his arms and covering her with kisses.

She knew that the desire rising inside her could only be quenched by total surrender to David's passionate lovemaking. She lost all sense of time. There was no tomorrow, no yesterday. . .only the present was real.

CHAPTER TEN

WHEN she awoke, David had gone. Melissa stretched languorously in the huge bed, her hand reaching out to touch the place where he had lain beside her after they had made love. He had told her how much he'd come to rely on her being there, how he couldn't imagine life without her now. He had said so many tender words to her...everything but the one sentiment she had hoped to hear... those three important little words... I love you.

She pulled herself upright and leaned back against the soft pillows. She had to admit that their lovemaking was pure magic, but what she longed for now was some sign of commitment on David's part. She wanted to be more than his soulmate, helpmate...the person he turned to when the going got tough and he needed sympathy. She needed a feeling of security about their relationship. She wanted to know that David wouldn't just walk out on her.

Oh, God! The very thought of it happening to her was too awful to contemplate. David had said he had come to rely on her...but she knew that without David her whole life would change. He'd become the centre of her universe. Maybe it was time to try a different tack. Perhaps if she made herself less available...

Determinedly she jumped out of bed and began to get ready for the day ahead.

Deal with each situation as it comes, she told herself firmly, as she went down in the lift. She knew she couldn't change David's independent character. . .nor should she try!

He moved forward to meet her when she arrived in the hotel lobby. His eyes held a look of proprietorial post-seduction as he bent to touch the tightly wound chignon on the top of her head.

'Back to business, is it, Sister?' he asked playfully.

'David, please don't undo those pins,' she pleaded, eyeing him cautiously as his hands hovered above her head. 'It's taken me ages to fix that chignon this morning.'

'I know; I've been waiting down here, wondering what was happening.' He smiled down at her. 'Look what was waiting for me at the desk!'

Melissa took the slip of paper. It was a telephone message received during the night.

'The receptionist decided we would be asleep, so she asked the caller to leave a message,' David said quietly.

Melissa smiled. 'So Mark wanted to contact us. This says he might come out to our island some time. It's a bit vague.'

David laughed. 'It's a step in the right direction.' He put a hand under her arm. 'I'm glad they didn't disturb us during the night.'

She felt the blush rising to her cheeks. 'Have you paid the bill?' she asked, quickly turning away from him.

He nodded. 'Let's go and collect our patients.'

* * *

Pulau Tanu looked like home to Melissa as the helicopter circled over the landing pad before making a rapid, noisy descent. The palm trees seemed to be rushing up to meet her as she looked out of the window. The sun shining on the turquoise blue sea made her think of the warm swims she would have each morning, the cool of the night strolls along the beach with David and. . .

She frowned as her romantic thoughts dissipated. The little figure waiting for them on the tarmac was waving happily. Jenny was obviously pleased to see them back. Well, to see David back, she corrected herself.

A familiar sinking feeling arrived in the pit of her stomach and she had to admit that she was jealous. . .and mystified by the whole unpleasant situation of David, Jenny, Victor and young Paul. In Singapore she had been able to shelve the problem, but here on the island, as long as Jenny stayed, it would be impossible to forget the enigma.

As Melissa walked across the concrete towards Jenny she fixed a smile on her face. Mustn't let her know her true feelings! She noticed the stern expression on David's face as Jenny ran towards him. Was he too hiding his real feelings? Did that inhospitable expression on his face hide the way he really felt about Jenny?

During the weeks that followed, Melissa was often to question David's real feelings. He continued to show little or no friendliness towards Jenny, but it was apparent to Melissa that there was some secret they both shared.

She tried not to attach too much importance to the fact that David's attitude to herself had changed since they had arrived back from Singapore. She wondered if it was because they were never alone together; he was obviously reluctant to allow the other staff to witness any show of affection between them.

But she longed for him to make some advances towards her again. Surely they could arrange to meet each other alone, away from the prying eyes.

But it seemed that David didn't share her desire to progress with their relationship. Even if she'd decided to play it cool with him he wouldn't have noticed! Their sole contact was in the clinic, working together with the patients.

It was true their early morning swims often coincided, but David made a point of keeping his distance in the sea, and there were no romantic idylls on the sand afterwards.

But worst of all was the constant presence of Jenny. Whenever Melissa set foot outside her cabin, Jenny appeared from her own cabin next door. It was impossible to avoid her and the constant reminder of the unpleasant situation.

There was nothing for it but to throw herself wholeheartedly into her medical work so that she had no time to brood. A month had passed since their flying visit to Singapore, and she was pleased to hear that their pneumonectomy patient was returning for convalescence with the full approval of the surgeon.

As she heard the sound of the helicopter droning over the sea, she left the clinic and walked along, pushing a wheelchair to wait for her patient. After a couple of minutes she heard David sprinting along behind her, but didn't turn round.

'Let's hope we get it right this time,' she said quietly as he came alongside her.

'Oh, there'll be no problems this time,' he reassured her. 'I've had a long chat on the phone with the surgeon at NUH. He's very confident now. All the patient needs is rest, relaxation and good general nursing care. How are your staff shaping up now?'

She smiled. 'Very well. The early problems have been sorted out.'

'Well done! Keep up the good work.'

Melissa thought he sounded like a teacher speaking to a pupil. She almost expected him to pat her on the head! She'd had a number of problems with the young inexperienced Malay nurses at first, but she had been patient with them, and now her patience was being rewarded. She could come out of the clinic, at a moment's notice, knowing that the place would be running smoothly in her absence. Yes, she had to admit that she was fully in control of her professional life. . .which was some consolation!

The huge iron bird touched down on the helicopter pad. The doors opened and the patient was helped down to the waiting wheelchair.

'Welcome back to Tanu, Geoff!' said David, holding out his hand.

The patient smiled happily. 'Thanks, Doctor. I've got a message for you.'

David looked puzzled. 'A message?' he queried.

'From your brother.'

Melissa saw the look of excitement on David's face as he asked the patient to explain.

Geoff Collier cleared his throat nervously as he delivered his important message. 'Your brother told me to tell you that he'd be coming out here soon, so long as he didn't get stopped again.'

David frowned. 'How do you mean, stopped?'

'They stopped him from getting on the helicopter this morning. He'd told the doctor at the clinic he was your brother and you'd invited him to come out here. But there was a big argument about something at the last minute. Well, you've got to admit that he doesn't look much like you, Doctor,' the patient finished off. 'Basically, I don't think anyone believed his story.'

'But surely he had his passport?' David queried impatiently.

'Yes, I believe he had,' Geoff Collier said. 'But I remember the pilot saying he wanted to check up on it. He said the photo didn't look anything like the man who said he was your brother. That was when the young man lost his temper and said. . .well, he said rather too much! There was no way now that the pilot was going to bring him along.'

Melissa gave a wry grin. 'I can imagine the whole scene! It must surely have been Mark.'

'Oh, I believed him,' Geoff Collier put in hurriedly. 'He only needs a shave and a change of clothing to make him look presentable, I would say. Anyway, he called out to me and told me to tell you he'll be out within the next few days or not at all.'

'Well, that's very comforting!' David said in a dry tone. He turned to look at Melissa. 'Come on, let's get Geoff settled in the clinic. I want to run some tests on him this afternoon, so that we know exactly what's going on.'

Melissa sensed the disappointment and anxiety that David was experiencing again, as they wheeled their patient back to the clinic. Every time that a reunion seemed possible there was some problem to prevent it.

When she had settled Geoff Collier in one of the upstairs rooms at the clinic, she helped David with the tests. The clinical notes the patient had brought with him gave them most of the details they needed, but David was a stickler for checking everything. He wanted to make his own medical notes based on his own clinical tests and observations.

At the end of the afternoon David was satisfied with his results and confident enough to leave Sister Watson in charge of their patient.

It was time for their round of the in-patients at the clinic. Melissa had found that the patients looked forward to this time of the day when they could air their grievances and ask questions about their treatment. On the odd occasion when she and David had been too busy to do the round, there had been numerous complaints.

But this evening they had finished their work and could relax with the patients, listening and advising. Melissa's eyes strayed to the window, as she watched David examining one of the overweight patients who was drastically reducing.

'We can't increase the pace any more,' David was telling the tense executive. 'You're doing extremely well, but it would be foolish to. . .'

His words droned on as, through the window, Melissa watched the darkening sky. The brief twilight had exploded in a beautiful display of orange and crimson. And now all the bright colours were disappearing. She couldn't see through the trees, but she knew the kaleidoscope would vanish below the horizon, leaving a fleeting trail of colour over the sea.

'. . . Don't you think so, Sister?' David asked her.

She turned back from the window. 'I'm sorry, I missed the question.'

David frowned. 'I was saying that a rapid weight loss can be dangerous. I've no intention of reducing the calorie intake any further.'

Melissa stepped forward. 'Yes, Dr Sanderson is quite right. And we're all so pleased with your progress, Mr Johnson.'

She flashed the patient a bright smile and some of his tension appeared to ease.

'I've got this important sales conference in two weeks, but I suppose I could stay on until a couple of days before,' he told them.

'Yes, why don't you do that?' said Melissa, in a sympathetic voice.

They went out into the corridor and she made a beeline for the balcony. 'I've got to get some air, David. That's the last patient, so if you don't need me any more I'll go off duty. Shirley Watson is on tonight.'

'Are you coming in to supper?' he asked, walking behind her to the balcony.

She pushed open the long windows and stepped

outside. 'Probably not. I'm not hungry...just hot and tired.

'You ought to have something to eat,' he said firmly, his eyes searching hers as he looked down at her.

She laughed, feeling the relative cool of the evening restoring her spirits. 'You're always exhorting people to eat! I'm OK... I'll pick up a sandwich from the kitchen.'

'Make it two,' he said. 'And I'll get a bottle of wine.'

'But what about supper in the dining-room? I mean...the patients like to chat and...'

'Mike Brent can be in charge tonight. It's time we gave him more responsibility. He's specialising in psychotherapy, so it'll be good for him to talk to his patients in an off-duty situation. I've tended to treat him like a junior houseman. He's thirty-one, for heaven's sake! At his age I was a consultant.'

'You mean four years ago?' asked Melissa, in a bantering tone.

David gave a dry laugh. 'Heavens! It is only four years, isn't it? The longest four years of my life.'

'Why do you say that?' she asked.

He hesitated. 'Mark dropped out four years ago. I've been trying to contact him ever since...but every time I got close, he avoided me. Can you imagine what it's like when your own brother hates you?'

Melissa put out a hand and touched his arm in a gesture of sympathy. She couldn't put into words the sentiments she would like to express, so she evaded the issue.

'I'll go and get the sandwiches,' she told him. 'My place or yours?'

His stern face eased into a boyish grin. Melissa realised it was over a month since they had had one of their romantic suppers on one of the moonlit verandas down by the sea. But they were picking up where they left off.

'Let's make it yours,' he said softly. 'It's high tide soon and your veranda is directly over the sea. We'll be able to dive off the end.'

A sudden unpleasant thought struck her. 'David, you realise that Jenny will be round as soon as she sees us?'

'Oh, no, she won't. I've asked her to have supper in Victor's room tonight. Sister Watson told me he was feeling a bit under the weather...so we'll be quite alone.'

Melissa smiled to herself as she ran down the stairs and across to the kitchen. A whole romantic evening to themselves! But why did David think it necessary to get rid of Jenny before this sort of evening could be arranged? Why did he never show her any affection when Jenny was there? It was almost as if he was trying to keep the two of them happy.

No, that can't be true! she told herself hurriedly as she waited for the cook to make up some chicken sandwiches. David couldn't be two-timing her...could he?

'No need to wait, *madame*,' the cook interrupted her thoughts. 'I will send the maid to your cabin. Two plates, yes?'

'Thank you.' Melissa smiled as she turned away.

'Some fruit, *madame*? Your doctor likes fruit.'

Heavens she thought. The cat would be out of the bag now if the staff were calling David 'her doctor'. Perhaps she should simply have smuggled the sandwiches across as they used to.

David was impressed with the candlelit setting as he climbed up the wooden stairs to her veranda.

'I can see you had some help,' he remarked as he glanced at the white starched tablecloth, the vase of fresh-cut flowers, little side bowls of salad and gleamingly polished wine glasses. There was even an ice bucket for the wine. 'I thought we were going to have one of our picnics.'

'So we were,' she said lightly. 'But they were being extra helpful in the kitchen, and one thing led to another. Look, I hope you don't mind that the staff know about. . .that we're having a quiet little supper together.'

'Mind? Why should I mind?' He was putting the wine into the ice bucket. Suddenly he reached across and took hold of her by the shoulders, pulling her towards him. 'It's been so long since we were alone together.'

She heard the rasping urgency of his voice as he pressed her against his hard muscular chest. She thought she could feel his heart thumping as madly as her own as she closed her eyes in anticipation of his caresses. She felt his kiss on her lips and responded with a deep longing. Yes, it had been a long time since they'd been alone together. . .too long. . .but tonight. . .

She tensed as she heard Jenny's brittle voice calling to them from out of the darkness.

'I heard you were having a party.'

David released Melissa as suddenly as he had swept her into his arms. Melissa couldn't believe the transformation from the ardent lover to this cool, poised, indifferent man. He was obviously anxious that Jenny shouldn't witness anything that might indicate they were close.

'I thought you were supposed to be looking after Victor,' he said evenly, as the diminutive blonde appeared in the candlelight.

'Oh, how romantic it all looks!' Jenny climbed up the stairs and sat down in one of the wicker chairs. 'I'd love a glass of wine.'

Melissa bridled. 'Jenny, David asked you about Victor.'

Jenny smiled unconcernedly. 'Oh, he's all right. Whenever he wants a bit of attention he has one of his funny turns, poor old thing. I've asked Sister to give him a sleeping pill.' She reached towards the table and picked up an empty glass. 'David, be an angel—I'm dying for a drink. . .'

Melissa turned on her heel and walked to the other end of the veranda. Staring out into the sea, she counted up to ten. . .and then twenty! The wretched woman couldn't be that thick! She must know that she was breaking up a cosy little *diner à deux*.

She turned round to give her friend a piece of her mind, but found herself completely thrown by the fact that David was actually pouring out two glasses of wine and handing one to Jenny!

'Have you got another glass, Melissa?' he asked nonchalantly.

If looks could kill, David would have been dead! But Melissa realised that he wasn't even looking at her now. He was engrossed in conversation with her uninvited guest, looking as if nothing untoward had occurred.

Fuming inwardly, she found another glass, placed it on the table and waited. David needn't think she was going to pour her own wine!

'Would you pass me one of those chicken sandwiches?' Jenny was saying. 'I think the kitchen staff thought I was on Victor's low-calorie diet tonight. I'm starving!'

The sandwiches, fruit and salad disappeared quickly, but Melissa ate very little. She was biding her time until Jenny left them alone again. The tide was high and the waves had started to lap up against her veranda. It was the perfect time for a moonlight swim.

'I'm afraid I'll have to leave you girls,' David suddenly announced. 'Thanks for the supper, Melissa.'

She swallowed hard. How could he walk off like this? The unfeeling brute!

Outwardly she remained calm and poised. She wouldn't let him see how disappointed she was!

'That's nice,' said Jenny, as soon as they were alone. 'We can have a little heart-to-heart chat.'

'Jenny, I don't want a little chat!' Melissa tried to modify her indignation but failed. 'You had no right to come here breaking up my supper party with David. I know he felt exactly the same about it, but he's too much of a gentleman to express his annoyance to you.'

Jenny dissolved into peals of apparently helpless laughter.

Melissa frowned. 'What's so funny?'

'You are! Imagining that David is in love with you. What's taking him so long to declare his intentions, then? Why does he go around looking so worried if he's in love with you?'

'Jenny, you simply don't understand David. If he's been looking worried recently it's because he's anxious about his younger brother. I don't suppose you know about Mark, but. . .'

'I know about Mark!' Jenny's expression was one of contempt as she stared across at Melissa in the flickering candlelight. 'You forget that I knew David intimately four years ago. We had no secrets from each other. I know how Mark hates David. . .and quite right too!'

'Why do you say that?' asked Melissa, disturbed by the passionate look on Jenny's face. This couldn't be another lie. . .this had got to be the truth.

'David ruined Mark's life,' Jenny declared.

'No, you're wrong.' Melissa's defence of David was automatic. She couldn't believe the worst of him. 'He's been trying to find Mark. We saw him in Singapore, and he's promised to come out here soon for a reunion with David.'

'Out here?' Jenny's voice wavered incredulously. 'Mark is coming here?'

'Yes, any day now. He should have come today, but he was turned away from the helicopter. He doesn't look as if he could possibly be David's brother. He's thin and scruffy-looking. . .'

'David did that to him,' Jenny said in an ominous tone. 'Mark will never forgive him. He's not coming for a reunion. . .he's coming for revenge.'

'But what did David do?' Melissa persisted. 'Was it something to do with the girl Mark was in love with?'

Jenny gave her a brief, pitying smile. 'Ah, so you know about that. Of course it was to do with the girl. Isn't there always a girl involved where David is concerned?'

'Well, go on. . .what happened?' Melissa prompted, breathlessly.

'David wanted her for himself. . .and what David wants, he always gets.'

CHAPTER ELEVEN

MELISSA awoke next morning with a distinct feeling of disquiet. Her disturbing conversation with Jenny still lingered on in her mind. It was so difficult to separate fact from fiction where Jenny was concerned, but if there was a grain of truth in what she'd said about the rift between David and his brother Mark, then the implications were more serious than she thought.

She shivered as she remembered the desolate haunted look in Mark's eyes. She'd never seen a young man who looked as if he'd been to hell and back. But David couldn't be responsible for that, could he? There were always two sides to every story.

She sat up in bed and her eyes strayed over to the fantastic view of the beach. She always slept with the wooden shutters wide open so that she could hear the sound of the sea and take advantage of the cooling sea breezes. Through the window she caught sight of David's lean, athletic body diving into the waves. Maybe this was a good time for a swim!

She made for the edge of the breakers and swam through to the calmer water beyond. David was swimming back towards the shore, but he changed his direction and came towards her.

'Sorry I had to leave you two together last night,'

he told her with a wry grin. 'I know how much you enjoy Jenny's company.'

She trod water as she eyed him speculatively. 'You're not sorry at all. You don't like hearing Jenny's fictitious innuendoes.'

He laughed, but Melissa noticed that his dark, sardonic eyes remained serious. 'You could be right. But I think we've heard all she's got to say and discounted it, haven't we?'

Melissa moved suddenly towards him so that she was close enough to watch his reaction. 'I don't think we've heard everything. Last night, she told me that you were responsible for Mark going away and. . .'

'Why were you talking about Mark?'

David's voice was icy cold and his eyes hostile.

'I simply told Jenny that Mark was coming out here for a reunion and. . .'

'You told her Mark was coming to the island?' he repeated evenly.

Melissa turned on to her front and began striking out for the shore in a vigorous breast-stroke. 'If you're going to keep interrupting me you'll never hear the full story.'

She was aware that he had caught up with her as she heard his increased breathing beside her. She turned her head towards him.

'Now, do you want to hear what Jenny told me?'

'No, I don't! It's all a pack of lies.'

She watched him streaking through the water in front of her, making for the shore. If only she could believe him! If only she could be confident that what

Jenny had hinted at had only taken place in her imagination.

She reached the shore as David was disappearing into his cabin. There was definitely no romance in the air this morning! she thought, as she sprinted up the beach. Perhaps it might be an idea if she called in on Jenny to clarify a few points...see if she could trip her up on her story! What had sounded plausible last night seemed unlikely in the cold light of day.

Melissa showered, put on her uniform and went round to Jenny's cabin. The door was wide open. She called Jenny's name and went inside. The bed hadn't been slept in and there was no sign of Jenny.

Where on earth had the wretched girl slept? she wondered.

She went back on to the veranda and saw David coming out of his cabin next door.

'Jenny didn't sleep here last night,' she told him. Any idea where she might be?'

He frowned. 'Probably in Victor's room at the clinic. They put another bed in there, you know.'

She nodded, feeling a sense of relief.

'Why do you want to see her?' asked David.

'Just checking up on something,' she replied lightly.

'Look, why don't we go to Victor's room and check up together? I suppose you're wanting her to repeat her story?'

Melissa gave him a rueful smile. 'Something like that.'

He smiled back. 'God, you're incorrigible! Come on.'

He put his hand under her elbow and began to steer her over in the direction of the clinic. As they walked, she could smell the morning-fresh odour of his newly showered skin mingled with the faint tang of the salty sea. A *frisson* of sensual arousal ran through her. It was true...he was irresistible! How could any girl fail to be won over by him if he decided to seduce her?

She tried to think rationally again as they arrived at the clinic. She must keep a clear head and not be swayed by Jenny's accusations against David.

Victor's door was ajar. David pushed it wide open and they went in. Melissa could see at once that the second bed in Victor's room hadn't been slept in.

'Where's Jenny?' asked David.

'Haven't seen her this morning,' Victor replied. 'Isn't she in her cabin?'

'Did you see her last night?' Melissa asked quickly.

'Not after supper...look, what's this all about?'

'Nothing to worry about,' David put in. 'Melissa wanted to have a word with her about something. How are you feeling today, Victor?'

'I'm feeling better than I did last night,' Victor replied uncertainly. 'The chest pains went away while I was asleep.'

'I'm just going to take your blood-pressure,' David told him, giving Melissa a knowing look.

She understood at once that he was wanting to keep their patient occupied while she continued her search for Jenny.

'I'll be back soon,' she said as she went out into the corridor.

Going immediately to the reception desk, she asked the nurse on duty if she had seen Jenny.

'Yes, she was in here earlier,' the girl replied. 'She got herself a lift on the helicopter. She left this letter for her husband.'

Jenny remembered hearing the early helicopter. In fact that was what had wakened her this morning.

'But did she say why she was going. . .when she was coming back?'

'I think it's all in the letter, Sister,' the nurse replied in a diplomatic voice. 'Oh, she did say something about missing her little boy.'

'Well, she has been away from him rather a long time,' Melissa put in, although privately she couldn't remember one occasion when Jenny had mentioned that she was missing young Paul. In fact, Melissa had come to the opinion that Jenny was totally devoid of maternal instinct!

'I'll take the letter in to Victor,' she said, holding out her hand. 'I think he may need some help in absorbing the contents.'

The young Chinese nurse hesitated. 'I'm sorry, Sister, but Mrs Linden said I wasn't to give him the letter until tonight.'

'Tonight?' Melissa echoed. 'But the poor man will be beside himself with worry by then! We can't have an angina patient getting himself worked up.'

The nurse's response was to seize the envelope and put it in a drawer. 'I'm sorry, Sister, but I promised.'

For an instant Melissa thought of pulling rank on the girl, but then she realised that she had put her in an invidious position. A promise was a promise. They'd just have to placate Victor until the evening.

As soon as she got David by himself, she began to explain the situation. They were standing outside their pneumonectomy patient's room, and David turned to look at her, his hand already on the doorknob.

'You can't be serious! She went on the helicopter? Maybe she's gone to Singapore to do some shopping.'

Melissa took a deep breath. 'Nurse Chang told me that Jenny claimed to be missing her little boy. . .she wanted to go back home.'

The dark brown eyes were hostile as David stared down at her. 'But that's ridiculous! Look, did you upset Jenny last night? What did you say to her that might have made her want to leave here?'

As he was speaking, he moved away from the door, taking hold of Melissa's arm and leading her to the end of the corridor.

'Of course I didn't upset Jenny!' she flung at him. 'She was the one who upset me, with talk about how you'd ruined Mark's life!'

A veiled, guarded look came into his eyes. 'So that's what she said, is it? And did you believe her?'

She turned away from him, unable to look up into those eyes that had once held such tenderness for her. 'I don't know what to believe any more. She said there was a girl. . . Mark wanted her. . .you wanted her. . .so there was no contest.'

'I wondered when she'd tell you that one,' David said quietly. 'Look, we can't talk about it now. Let's leave it till Mark gets here. See what he has to say about what happened.'

'If Mark gets here,' Melissa said pointedly.

'Oh, I think he'll come, just as I think Jenny will come back from her Singapore shopping trip on this afternoon's helicopter and...'

'No, she won't,' Melissa interrupted. 'She wrote a note for Victor. The nurse had to promise not to give it to him until tonight.'

'Oh, God!' David moved away from her and stood looking out of the louvred windows towards the forest. 'By then it will be too late to stop her. She'll be checking in for the night flight back to the UK... I wonder if I could have her stopped at the airport. Perhaps if I went over I could persuade her to come back.'

Melissa stared up at him, unable to believe her ears. 'But I thought you didn't like having her out here. From the minute she arrived you've been hostile towards her...most of the time...'

Her voice trailed away as she had a sudden mental image of David and Jenny standing together here in the corridor, by this very window. And David hadn't been hostile then...not when he thought he and Jenny were alone. His voice had been oh, so tender when Melissa overheard him telling Jenny they couldn't live in the past. And the kiss on Jenny's forehead had been real enough.

'What do you mean, most of the time?' David asked her evenly.

She moved away, walking back towards their patient's room. She could never admit that she had spied on them, albeit unintentionally.

'Let's get on with the work,' she said firmly.

He caught up with her and put his hand on her arm. 'You're holding something back, Melissa. Come on, out with it!'

'I'm not holding back as much as you!' she retorted. 'Why this sudden interest in Jenny now that she's left us? Why do you want to get her back? I would have thought you'd be glad to be rid of her.'

'I would have preferred her to stay, for reasons I can't explain at the moment. I wish you hadn't interfered with my plans, but. . .'

'I haven't done anything! It's not my fault your wretched girlfriend has taken off!'

'If that's what you think, then there's nothing more to be said.'

David pushed open the door to their patient's room and went in. His suddenly total professional manner helped Melissa to assume her professional role again, but she longed to continue her argument with him. As far as she was concerned there was a lot more to be said on all sides!

David sounded their patient's chest with his stethoscope and smiled reassuringly. 'I think it would be a good idea if Sister took you out on to the sea-shore today, Geoff. The change will do you good.'

He turned to look down at Melissa, his eyes devoid of all emotion. 'Perhaps you could arrange that, Sister. Take a porter to push the wheelchair—I don't want to tire you in this heat. I'm going to see Victor Linden to put his mind at rest and then I'm going to request the helicopter to take me over to Singapore. I want to be at Changi Airport this evening.'

Melissa turned away. 'As you wish, sir,' she said coldly, 'But I hope you know what you're doing.'

The sand beneath Melissa's sandalled feet felt hot and there wasn't a breath of air as she asked the porter to move her patient under the palm trees. Up above the sea she could hear the droning of an approaching helicopter.

So David had been successful in his request for transport to Singapore, she thought resignedly. He must want to get Jenny back pretty badly!

A few yards away, under the trees, Mike Brent, the Australian doctor, was holding a psychotherapy session with half a dozen intense executives from England. Melissa noticed that in the couple of weeks they had been here, the men had become more relaxed, lost the necessary weight and gained a healthy-looking suntan. But from the sound of the problems that they were trying to iron out at the moment it seemed they had a long way to go.

She looked at her patient. He was leaning back in his chair, his mouth open as he snored gently. The porter too was leaning against a tree, his eyes glazed over in a soporific state. She kicked off her sandals and sat down on the sand as she asked herself if she had really found her tropical paradise.

The helicopter was taking off again, flying away into the distance, taking David to see his ex-girlfriend. . .or his girlfriend, whichever way she liked to think of it.

No, she had to admit, they had all brought their own problems to this tropical paradise, problems that it was impossible to escape from even in these idyllic surroundings.

It had seemed like a long day since David had left her. As the night fell on the clinic Melissa felt relieved. She had been feeling sorry for Victor, having to fob him off with stories of Jenny going over to Singapore to do some shopping. Melissa knew that he had only half believed her, but he had become resigned to Jenny's impulsive nature and knew it was best not to ask too many questions.

Melissa was longing to see what Jenny had written in the letter, but David had forbidden her to open it until he had telephoned her from Singapore.

When the nurse at the desk told her there was a call for her she hurried out of Victor's room, not wanting her patient to overhear the critical conversation.

David's voice at the other end sounded flat and despondent. 'I tried, Melissa, but Jenny wouldn't agree to come back with me.'

It was a difficult line, with too much noise in the background. 'David, I can hardly hear you. Where are you?'

'I'm still at the airport. Jenny has just left me to go through passport control. You'd better give Victor the letter. . .but make sure you're there when he opens it. And have some amyl nitrate ready just in case.'

'Of course. . .when will you be back?'

'Tomorrow.'

The line was still crackling. Melissa put the phone down and turned to the nurse at the desk.

'Nurse Chang, I'd like to give Mr Linden his letter now,' she said.

The Oriental eyes remained inscrutable as the letter was handed over.

Melissa took the letter. 'Thank you, Nurse.' She moved away and went back to Victor's room. Her eyes strayed across to the treatment trolley. Yes, everything was ready in case Victor had a sudden attack of angina.

She went across to Victor's bedside and sat down on the chair. Gently she began to tell him that there was a possibility that Jenny had decided to go back to England to see little Paul.

'You know how Jenny misses her son,' she improvised, her hand firmly holding the patient's.

Victor looked alarmed. 'But Jenny wouldn't just walk out without saying anything. And I don't think she misses Paul all that much. She's not what you'd call the maternal type.'

'She's actually written you a letter.' Melissa reached into her pocket.

Feeling miserable and helpless, she watched while her patient read Jenny's letter. She waited until he tossed it across the sheet towards her.

'She says she's homesick, but I don't believe her,' Victor said flatly. 'She's up to something. . .but I don't know what.'

Melissa squeezed the patient's hand as she scanned the brief note.

'Why couldn't she have discussed it with me?' Victor was lamenting.

'Perhaps she didn't want to upset you,' Melissa

suggested, hating to have to make such fatuous statements.

Her patient leaned back on his pillows. 'It's a long time since I allowed Jenny to upset me. No, I'm immune to her machinations now. You know, I didn't even love her when we got married. It was a marriage of convenience. We both needed something from the other. . . Paul isn't my child. . . Jenny was already pregnant.'

Melissa felt a cold shiver running down her spine. That was exactly what Jenny had told her. So that bit of the story must be true. And if it were true that they'd made a marriage of convenience, wasn't it likely that the rest of the saga held a ring of truth?

'You've taken it better than I thought you would, Victor,' she said evenly. 'Is there anything I can get you before I settle you down for the night?'

'Yes, bring me some notepaper. I want to write a letter,' Victor replied tonelessly.

CHAPTER TWELVE

DAVID returned the next morning. Melissa was working in the treatment-room when she heard the helicopter overhead. Her concentration wavered from the task in hand and she dropped the pair of forceps she was lifting from the steriliser. A distinctly unladylike epithet escaped her lips.

'Is everything all right, Sister?' Nurse Chang asked, coming up behind her and picking up the now unsterile forceps. 'Let me help you.'

'Thanks.' Melissa watched as the nurse took the forceps to the sink and began to wash them before placing them on the tray of unsterile items waiting for sterilisation. Her eyes strayed to the window as the helicopter engines ceased.

'I'm going to go out and help with the arrival of the new patients, Nurse Chang,' Melissa said.

She knew she wasn't fooling anybody as she escaped through the open door of the clinic. There was a certain amount of speculation going on about her relationship with David. She had gone into rooms where the conversation had dried immediately on several occasions.

She found herself wondering if the kitchen staff had started the rumours. They might have discussed how her romantic supper with David had been interrupted by the untimely arrival of Jenny. She remembered how the maid had averted her eyes when she came to collect the plates, but Melissa knew the girl couldn't fail to have noticed that David had gone and Jenny had stayed. And anyone walking in the vicinity would have heard their raised voices!

There was also the fact that Jenny had mysteriously flown off the next morning without even telling her husband. Melissa knew that Nurse Chang would have embroidered on that one to all her friends. . .especially the bit about the letter. How she must have loved reporting that she'd countermanded Sister's orders!

Melissa walked quickly through the trees to the helicopter pad. The bright rays of the morning sun were already hot as she emerged from the shade and walked across the scorching concrete to the helicopter.

David was climbing down; she saw the dejected look on his face. Oh, God! she thought. Did Jenny mean so much to him?

He smiled when he saw her. 'Only one patient today, but it's good of you to meet us.'

'All in the line of duty,' she said, in a totally professional voice, before turning away to concentrate all her attention on the new patient.

The middle-aged, overweight man was looking around him appraisingly. 'What a tropical paradise!' he said. 'I didn't know places like this still existed on our overcrowded planet. I'm going to love being here.'

'Well, that's half the treatment over with, if you think you're going to enjoy yourself,' Melissa told him. 'I'll take you along to the clinic for a full medical check-up and then we'll settle you in your room.'

She glanced down at the case notes. 'Mr Robert Douglas, welcome to the Tanu clinic. I'm glad your first impressions are favourable. Now, I see from the notes that you're simply here for rest, relaxation, exercise and weight loss, so a cabin near the sea will be what you need.'

'Sounds wonderful! You're so lucky, working in a place like this.'

'Yes, aren't we,' David put in. 'There's absolutely nothing more we could ask for.'

Melissa's eyes met David's for a brief instant and she thought she saw the pain of his concealed emotions.

But she was trying so hard not to feel sorry for him. He had brought all this on himself. They could have been happy together if he had been honest with her. If only he'd told her the truth. . .but what was the truth?

They escorted their new patient through the trees to the clinic and took him into one of the treatment-rooms for a thorough check-up before settling him into one of the cabins close to the sea.

'It's a pity about the high blood-pressure and high cholesterol level,' David said to Melissa as they walked back along the beachside path. 'He's got such infectious *joi de vivre*. The sort of man who gives the impression he hasn't got a care in the world.'

Melissa nodded as she looked across to Mike Brent's psychotherapy group under the trees. 'He's not the sort of man to need psychiatric counselling,' she agreed.

David shook his head. 'You can't judge a book by its cover, nor a patient by a first impression. It struck me that he could have some skeletons in his closet that might come out during his stay here.'

'There seems to be an epidemic of concealed skeletons at the moment,' Melissa remarked in a deliberately casual tone.

David appeared not to have heard her. He had stopped dead in his tracks and was looking out to sea, shading his eyes with his hand.

'Isn't that the fishing boat we came on?' he queried.

Melissa nodded. 'How could I ever forget! I didn't know they were still using it.'

'Oh, it's a cheap way of getting out here, even if it takes forever and you're at the mercy of the sea. . . I say, do you recognise that tall figure in front of the engine-room? Do you think it could possibly be. . .it is!'

David gave a boyish hoot of delight as he ran across the sand to meet the approaching boat.

So Mark had actually made it out here after all! Melissa pulled off her sandals and ran barefoot down the sandy beach to the water's edge.

She noticed how calm the sea was. There would be no need to rig up a landing pontoon this time, fortunately! She watched as the little landing boat put out to sea to bring back its one passenger.

Mark leapt out of the boat when he was some yards from the shore, wading through the shallows towards them.

Melissa smiled as she saw that he was still wearing the same shabby jeans, with their holes and patches. There was a saxophone case strapped to his back, but his only other luggage was a small duffel bag.

She hoped they would be able to equip him with whatever he needed. But most of all she hoped that the rift between the two brothers could be healed.

David was standing on the shore, his shoes in one hand, his stethoscope still around his neck, and a welcoming smile on his face.

'It's good to see you, Mark,' Melissa heard him say.

She saw David begin to extend his arms, tentatively, almost expecting a fraternal hug, but it was obvious the days of physical contact between the brothers had long since receded. There was not even a shaking of hands.

Mark walked past his brother towards Melissa. 'I've come for some of that food you promised me. Lord, I'm starving! Haven't had a decent meal for days.'

Melissa wanted to chide him for his rudeness towards his elder brother, but she knew that would serve no purpose at this stage. Maybe when Mark was feeling stronger he might be more amenable. She smiled and held out her hand. To her amazement, the young man took it and smiled back at her.

'Welcome to Tanu,' she said. 'We've been looking forward to seeing you again.'

Mark half turned to look at David. 'I'm sure you have,' he said through clenched teeth.

* * *

It took Melissa a couple of weeks to effect an improvement in Mark's behaviour. She was determined that he should be civil to David, at the very least, because until the brothers were able to communicate again, she knew there was little point in their so-called reunion.

As she sat out on her veranda one evening after supper she heard the sound of their voices in the next cabin and smiled to herself. It had been a wise move on her part to install Mark in Jenny's old cabin. That way both she and David could keep an eye on him. But it did also mean that she and David were overlooked whenever. . .or rather *if* ever they managed to get together on their own.

As she looked out across the darkened sea she had a sudden image of Jenny sitting beside her, telling her that Mark wasn't coming for a reunion, he was coming for revenge. It had certainly looked like that during the first few days of Mark's visit. But Melissa had stuck to her guns and made veiled hints to Mark, and even threats on some occasions, that whereas David might be willing to overlook his rudeness, she wasn't!

Mark and David's voices were coming closer now. She looked over the edge of her veranda. In the moonlight she could see that Mark was stripped to his bathing trunks, but David was still wearing the casual linen slacks and safari jacket he had put on for their supper with the patients in the dining-room.

'Mark's going for a swim, Melissa,' David called to her. 'But I said I preferred to sit on the veranda with you and discuss some of our patients. We've got a few problems to iron out, and there's never time during the day. Would that be convenient?'

'Of course. Anyway, we had a long swim before supper, so I haven't the strength to get in the water again.'

David was climbing the steps to her veranda as his brother made off into the sea.

'Did our swim tire you, Melissa?'

She noticed how David's voice had changed from the cool impersonal professional tone he adopted when they weren't alone and she wondered, as she so often did, why he wanted to keep their relationship secret. Because they still had a relationship, albeit not so passionately romantic as in the early days before Jenny broke up their idyllic life on the island. But since she had gone, David had mellowed again. . .but only when they were alone.

Melissa looked across now at the lean, muscular figure, sinking down into one of the deep armchairs on her veranda, remembering how he had pulled her into his arms at the end of their swim this evening. He had pressed his lips against hers and whispered that he couldn't live without her. But did that mean he loved her. . .or did it mean she was number one in his life until someone else took her place?

'I was tired before we swam out tonight,' she told him. 'And then we were rather energetic.'

He laughed. 'I hope that's an understatement. You were wonderful!'

She could feel her cheeks tingling and was glad that the light was dim! 'How about these patients you wanted to discuss, Doctor?' she asked primly.

'Oh, that was only a ploy to get you to myself. We've worked hard enough for one day. No, I wanted to ask you how you think Mark's getting along here. I mean, he's closer to you than anyone. You've worked wonders with him! I don't know how you've done it.'

She smiled. 'Well, it wasn't easy. There were times when I thought he was going to pick up his saxophone, pack his bag and walk out on us. The only thing that stopped him was his lack of money and the fact that it's difficult to walk off an island.'

'Yes, but how do you think he is, from a medical point of view?' David persisted.

Melissa looked surprised. 'Well, you're the doctor. You should know.'

'Oh, I'm not talking about physically. It's obvious he's putting on weight, and he looks so much better now you've trimmed that awful beard and persuaded him to use the shower again. But what's his mental health like? Do you think Mike Brent could do anything for him?'

She frowned. 'He doesn't need psychotherapy. . .does he?'

'I'm asking you what you think.'

She hesitated. 'Without knowing all the facts of the case I can't make a judgement. I mean, this girl who jilted him. . .'

There was the sound of footsteps pounding up the beach. Melissa paused in mid-sentence and her eyes looked beseechingly at David. 'We'll have to talk about this again. You must tell me the facts. . .'

Mark was running up the steps, his bare feet

dripping water on to the veranda. 'Lend me a towel, Melissa,' he said.

She went inside her cabin and tossed one out through the open window.

'Catch, Mark!'

'Thanks.' The young man rubbed at his long hair and beard before draping the towel around him. 'All I need now is a beer.'

'Well, I must go,' David said quickly.

Melissa, emerging from the interior with a tray of drinks, frowned. 'Wouldn't you like a drink, David?'

'No, thanks. Goodnight.'

As she looked across at David she thought he was trying to say something to her about Mark. Maybe he was leaving the coast clear so that she could check the younger brother's mental health. She sighed inwardly. It was a funny time to have a surreptitious psychotherapy session, but she'd have a go!

Mark had drunk a couple of beers before he began to open up and talk about himself. Melissa had played it cool, initially, chatting about everything except Mark's personal life. But now, when she began asking a few seemingly innocent questions, she could feel that he was happy to confide in her.

'So are you happy to be helping us out at the clinic?' she asked. 'I know you can only do the work that the orderlies do, but still it's a start. Doesn't it make you want to go back to your medical studies?'

Mark gave a bitter laugh. 'What, at twenty-five?'

'That's still young enough. Presumably you've got good qualifications to get you into a medical school.'

He took another drink from his can of beer. He had refused her offer of a glass, saying it tasted better from the can. 'Oh, sure. I could always pass the old exams. I just got disenchanted with the life of a student. I wasn't making any money, for a start, and that was playing havoc with my love life. I mean, what sort of girl fancies a bloke with no money?'

Melissa took a deep breath. 'Lots of girls don't care whether a man has money or not. Most girls make their own money nowadays, or else they're students like you were. And students all help each other out. I remember when. . .'

'Yes, but the girl I wanted loved money,' Mark interrupted with a fierceness that took Melissa by surprise. 'She told me she couldn't bear to be poor. That's why she left me. . .that and the fact that someone with more money came along and took her from me.'

'But it couldn't have just been the lack of money,' Melissa put in quickly. 'If this girl had really loved you for yourself, then she'd have stayed with you no matter what.'

Mark put his beer can down on the table and stood up. For a few minutes he paced the veranda without speaking. Melissa was beginning to get anxious, but she was sure she was on the right track. She was loath to break the silence. Any moment now, there could be a resolution to the problem.

The young man suddenly came back to the table and stared across at her with a sad haunted expression. 'You're probably right that it wasn't just the money. She couldn't have loved me, could she?'

'She might have thought she did at first,' Melissa said cautiously. Oh, why had David chickened out on this discussion? He knew all the facts and she was still floundering around in the darkness, trying to piece the jigsaw together. 'But then later on she. . .'

'Later on she fell for someone else, someone older, richer, with much better prospects than me,' he said in a low, ominous voice.

Melissa leaned across and put her hand over his. 'Whoever she was, she obviously wasn't worthy of you. I would say you were well rid of her.'

She realised at once that Mark had stopped listening to her. He was miles away in his own thoughts. It must have been, as David had told her, that this love affair hit Mark impossibly hard. She remembered how David had said that the girl had been the first female that Mark had ever loved. What were his words? The girl had taken the place of Mark's mother, sister, girlfriend. . .

'She was a lot older than me, much more sophisticated.' Mark's anguished voice broke into her thoughts. 'But how could he take Jenny away from me? My own brother!'

CHAPTER THIRTEEN

MELISSA went about her nursing duties the next morning as efficiently as she could, but her mind was on the damning accusation that Mark had made against David the night before. Over and over, during the night, as she had tossed and turned restlessly, unable to sleep, she'd told herself that there must be some mistake. David couldn't be the monster that he was made out to be. No one could be so cruel, so unfeeling!

She had deliberately not taken sides on the issue when Mark had made his accusation. She had remained silent so that she wouldn't say anything to which Mark might take exception. She was loath to break up the rapport that was building up between them. But she had also remained silent because she was in a state of shock! That the girl in question should have been Jenny had never occurred to her.

Whenever Jenny had tried to paint a bad picture of David, Melissa had forced herself to discount most of it. But to hear the story from Mark. . .

'You look as if you're miles away, Melissa. Will you be fit to assist me in Theatre in an hour?'

She jumped guiltily at the sound of David's voice. 'Yes, of course.'

He put a finger under her chin and tilted her face so that she had to look into his eyes. 'You're worried about something—I can see that. Is it Mark? What happened last night after I left? Did you find out how he's feeling?'

She looked around her. They were standing close together by the notice-board in the tiny staff-room. From the other side of the room she could see Nurse Chang watching her. The grapevine would soon be busy!

'David, we can't talk now,' she muttered, through clenched teeth.

'OK, then, as soon as we've finished operating. I think it's going to be a straightforward appendicectomy, no complications, so we'll be free this afternoon. How about a picnic on the other side of the island?'

She hesitated. The door opened and two more nurses had walked in, followed by Dr Mike Brent. Soon the entire staff would be watching them!

She forced herself to smile. 'Yes, that would be a good idea, and now, if you'll excuse me. . .'

Her heart was pounding as she went out and hurried along the corridor to supervise the theatre preparations. It was going to be difficult to get through the morning with David watching her every move.

She picked up the case notes to refresh her memory on the patient, a wealthy English businessman living in Kuala Lumpur. She remembered admitting him a couple of weeks ago, suffering from nervous fatigue. His doctor had recommended that he take some time off so that he could get away from the pressures of his business, hoping that this would improve his health. But it had transpired that he was suffering from chronic constipation. Out here on the island his diet had been changed and the constipation problem was improving. During the night, however, he had suffered from nausea and vomiting. David had examined him early this morning and noted that the generalised abdominal pain had become localised in the right iliac fossa. This, coupled with a rapid rise in temperature and pulse rate, had made him decide to operate.

Melissa put away the notes and went out into the ante-theatre to change into a surgical gown. A couple of Malay nurses closed the fastening at the back and tied the strings on her mask, before fixing her hair into a sterile cap. This was always the tricky bit!

She was waiting impatiently while the nurses fiddled when the swing doors opened and David walked in. His eyes twinkled with amusement as he watched.

She frowned into her mask. 'It's at times like this I consider having all my hair chopped off,' she muttered indistinctly.

David stepped forward, the eyes above his mask smiling. 'Don't you dare!' he whispered, so softly that she wasn't sure if she'd heard him right.

The nurses had stopped fiddling with her hair. She turned away, wondering why David was always at his most charming whenever she was contemplating making a clean break!

The nurses were holding open the swing doors to the theatre. Melissa went through and took her place across the table from David. The patient had been anaesthetised and the surgical team were waiting for them.

She handed David a scalpel and watched as he

made a small grid-iron incision starting just above the level of the anterior superior iliac spine. When he had isolated the enlarged appendix Melissa could see a faecalith obstructing the lumen of the appendix.

David looked up and spoke to the surgical team. 'The obstruction that we've found here has caused bacteria to multiply within the appendix and these have invaded its walls, causing obstruction to its blood supply. Our patient is going to feel a great deal more comfortable without this little appendage.'

Melissa leaned across to hold back the tissues with her retractors as David removed the appendix. When the wound had been closed and sutured, David moved away from the table, tossing his gloves into a bin.

'Thanks, everyone. You've been a good team.' He turned to smile at Melissa. 'You too, Sister! What would I do without you?'

She heard the murmur of voices and felt the familiar tingling in her cheeks beneath the mask. She wondered how everyone would react if they knew she was planning to break off this romantic relationship before it went any further.

David was waiting for her out in the corridor, his eyes full of tenderness. 'So how about this picnic?' he queried. 'How soon can you be ready?'

'David there's something I have to tell you,' she began, but he shook his head.

'Not now, Melissa. We've got all afternoon. We won't have to be back until the evening to check on this patient. Mike Brent and Shirley Watson will hold the fort. Besides, I want to hear all about your talk with Mark.'

'David, that's what I. . .'

But David was striding away from her. 'Later, Melissa. . . I've got to see a patient.'

The sea was as calm as a millpond when they set out in the old fishing boat. Melissa had thought she would never again want to set foot in the boat that had brought them over from the coast of Malaysia all those weeks ago. But when David had assured her that the sea was calm and that the captain had come over specially to take them out when David had radioed him, she agreed.

She found the presence of the Malay captain and a couple of sailors very comforting, because for the first time in her life she didn't want to be alone with David. In fact she didn't want to be alone with him ever again. This was going to be their farewell party, but only she was aware of the fact. It was going to be a wrench, but she couldn't carry on like this, torturing herself with thoughts of how David had double-crossed all of them.

She looked across at his muscular frame, outlined against the skyline as he stood in the bows. A soft breeze was ruffling his dark hair. He was wearing light brown shorts that showed off the muscles of his tanned legs to perfection. And the open-necked shirt displayed the dark hairs on his chest. She felt that he'd never looked more desirable!

But she had to remain strong. She mustn't be taken in by any more of his lies. What had Jenny said about him, all those weeks ago? That he was a womanising philanderer. Sadly, Melissa admitted to herself that she now had no alternative but to believe it was true.

Why on earth had she fallen so hopelessly in love with him, and, which was more to the point, why had she fallen for his pack of lies? He had always had an answer to all her accusations. His answers had tripped so lightly off his tongue. He'd probably rehearsed them in advance, knowing that someone would be sure to spill the beans sooner or later.

And the awful thing was that he didn't seem to care what he did. How could anyone who was in a caring profession like medicine be such a brute? He'd ruined his brother's life, made Jenny into a neurotic wreck and then turned his attentions on herself.

And she'd fallen for it hook, line and sinker!

The boat gave an unexpected lurch and she fell across the hard wooden seat. David turned round and moved back to sit beside her.

'Are you OK?' he asked, his eyes full of concern. 'You're not hurt?'

She shook her head. Oh no, she wasn't hurt outwardly, but she was bleeding inside.

'Soon be there,' he told her in a soothing voice. 'You're not a very good sailor, are you? I thought you'd be OK on a calm sea, but it's obvious you're suffering.'

He didn't know the half of it! Melissa sat up straight and looked out towards the approaching shore. They'd coasted the southern shore of the island and now they were coming in to land. Soon she would have to reveal that she knew everything.

She glanced up and saw David watching her. His eyes held such tenderness. Better make the most of these last few minutes of their friendship!

The captain dropped anchor some yards from the shore and let down a small lifeboat. David helped her over the side while the sailors organised the boxes and baggage.

The sand was a hot, dazzling white as they ran barefoot to the shelter of the palm trees.

'This is the place to have lunch,' David told her enthusiastically. 'But first, let's have a swim.'

He was already peeling off his shirt and removing his shorts to reveal the skin-tight black swimming pants that were so familiar to her.

'Come on, shake a leg!' He moved towards her, his fingers reaching for the buttons on her shirt, deftly unfastening the top two before she realised what was happening.

She stepped backwards in the sand. 'I can manage,' she said quickly. Now was the time to speak. . .now when he'd sensed that something was wrong. . .but she needed a swim first! She had to cool off after the boat journey, be in charge of all her faculties when she challenged David about the truth.

She saw the puzzled look in his eyes before she turned away to strip off her shirt and shorts. As she ran down the beach towards the water's edge, she acknowledged that she was guilty of procrastination. She was deliberately postponing the awful moment when she would shatter her own dreams of paradise on this island with David.

As she swam out from the shore, the tense feeling inside her began to evaporate. She decided that this was how a condemned man would feel when he was granted one last wish before execution.

Oh, don't be so silly! she told herself. There's no comparison between losing your life and losing the man you love. . .or is there?

As she cut through the breakers she realised that by now, she should be thinking of her love for David in the past tense. He should be the man she had loved.

He was swimming close beside her now, his eyes firmly fixed on the water.

'Melissa, come over here; underwater it's fantastic!'

Drawn by his boyish enthusiasm, she swam over to join him.

'Take a deep breath and go under the surface. . .like this. . .!'

She followed him beneath the surface of the water to the mysterious aquatic world below. Her problems dissolved as she watched the spectacular, multi-coloured tropical fish swirling around as if they were the background in some gigantic film set. The sea-bed below them was adorned with coral and pastel-coloured cushions of sea vegetation.

She returned to the surface gasping for air. David surfaced beside her, laughing with excitement.

'It's so beautiful in that magic world below!' he enthused. 'I'd like to be able to stay down there longer. We'll have to get ourselves some diving equipment next time we come out here. Take another deep breath and. . .'

'David, I'm hungry. Let's go back to shore,' she called, as she headed away from him. There wouldn't be a next time, so there was no point in making wild plans.

The captain and the sailors were spreading out the picnic food when Melissa got back to the shore. She thanked them and invited them to join her, but they declined, saying that they had their own food. They were going further into the trees where the shade was cooler.

David arrived back as she had put the finishing touches to the picnic. He sat down on the sand at the other side of the tablecloth that had been spread out over the sand.

'I hope the champagne is still cold,' he said, taking the bottle from the bucket of ice under the trees.

Trust David to bring champagne for the farewell picnic! Melissa thought as she automatically raised her glass to acknowledge his toast.

'To us!' David said softly.

She remained silent, feeling guilty that she should drink his champagne under false pretences. But then she reminded herself of all the pretence that he was guilty of and her own guilt disappeared.

Surprisingly, she found herself to be genuinely hungry as she started on the cold chicken, salad and rice. It had been a long morning; first her routine work in the clinic, the operation in Theatre, the boat journey and finally the swim. When she had eaten some of the chicken, she cut a piece of pineapple and leaned back against the palm tree behind her.

From the corner of her eye she saw that David had finished his meal. She watched him pushing away his plate, beginning to move towards her with that look in his eyes she had come to know...and love...so well!

A little voice inside her was saying, what does it matter what he's done in the past? Why can't you forget and begin afresh? But the rational side of her insisted that she could forgive him anything if he had only told her the truth. Lots of men like to play around with women. But David had invented a pack of lies. He had pulled the wool over her eyes too often, and for this she couldn't forgive him. Jenny had been right: David was not to be trusted where women were concerned.

'David, we have to talk!' She was surprised at the loudness of her voice. The words came out as if she were addressing a medical conference!

The tender expression in David's eyes vanished. 'That sounds ominous. It must have something to do with your discussion with Mark.'

She took a deep breath. 'Mark told me everything.'

'What exactly did my little brother tell you?' David's voice was icy cold.

Melissa gave a shiver of apprehension. 'He told me he'd been in love with Jenny...that you came along and took her from him.'

The silence that followed was broken only by the sound of the waves dashing on the shore. Melissa looked across at David, willing him to speak, as if by some magic he could erase the whole episode.

But he had risen to his feet, his eyes turned away from her looking out to sea, so that she couldn't read what thoughts were churning away inside him. When at last he spoke, his voice was low and husky, but devoid of emotion.

'I think it's time we went back to the clinic, Melissa.'

'David, you've got to tell me if it's true!' She leapt to her feet and flung herself at him, beating her hands against his muscular chest in frustration.

Firmly he removed her hands, looking down at her with an enigmatic expression. 'What do you believe, Melissa?' he asked coldly.

She hesitated. 'I have to believe the evidence. Three people have told me the same story. . . Jenny, Victor and Mark.'

'Victor? What did he tell you?'

'He told me that Jenny was pregnant when he married her. . .that it was a marriage of convenience, that. . .'

'OK, that's enough! I think you're enjoying putting the knife in!'

David was already bending down to pack the remains of the picnic in the boxes. Brusquely he called out for the sailors to come and help him. Melissa's hands moved automatically as she gathered her things together.

The desolate feeling in the pit of her stomach told her that it was finally over between them. She wondered if she could have ended it in a more amicable fashion, but came to the conclusion that a clean break was always painful.

The only course open to her now was to hand in her resignation and go back to England. She couldn't work alongside David again. . .not with all the memories of what might have been.

CHAPTER FOURTEEN

MELISSA looked at David from the other side of their post-operative patient's bed. Outwardly, he looked like the same man she had assisted that morning in theatre, but she knew that inwardly, like herself, a profound change had taken place. As he raised his head now from examining the appendix wound, his eyes were cold.

'Put a sterile dressing on this, Sister,' he said.

She nodded, turning away to pick up her forceps from the dressing trolley. When she turned back, David had moved on to the next patient. Melissa swallowed back the lump in her throat and got on with her work.

It was dark before she was able to escape from her duties and hurry back to her cabin. All the way, as she ran through the trees and then over the sandy path, she found herself remembering a conversation with David. They had discussed the fact that everyone should have a home they could hide in when they wanted to lick their wounds. Well, tonight her little cabin definitely felt like home.

Closing the door firmly behind her, she allowed the tears to fall. It had been such a strain holding them back. First the boat journey back with David, silent and morose, avoiding her eyes, and then the agony of working with him in the clinic. Being so close and yet so irrevocably far away from the only man she had ever loved.

She moved over to the bed and lay down on top of the sheet. Tomorrow she would hand in her resignation. David would have to manage without her until they found a replacement. Nurse Chang was perfectly capable of taking over Sister Watson's work, and that would mean the sister would be free to take over from her...

She could hear the sound of loud angry voices coming from the next cabin, and she pulled herself to a sitting position. It sounded as if David and Mark were having one hell of a row! And she had a pretty good idea what that would all be about.

At first she felt concerned for Mark. Maybe she should go round. And then, just as quickly as the row had started, it stopped. There was nothing but silence again. Only the sound of the waves on the shore and the gentle swish, swish, swish of the night breeze in the palm trees.

She wondered who had won the argument. More than likely they'd reached stalemate again and one of them had stormed off!

Melissa peeled off her damp uniform dress and headed for the shower. However the dispute had been resolved it now had nothing to do with her. She'd opted out for good.

She awoke to hear the morning helicopter leaving the island. Somehow she had managed to sleep for a short time during the night, but she was relieved to find it was daylight. She had a lot of preparations to make today, and the sooner she got started on the routine nursing work the better.

She dressed quickly and went out into the morning sunlight. The beach looked as idyllic as ever. She turned quickly away, heading towards the clinic. Pausing as she passed by Mark's open door, she wondered whether she should see how he was. After all, she was the one who had sparked off last night's row.

She went up the steps, calling his name. There was no answer, so she looked in through the doorway.

She felt she was re-enacting the scene when she had looked for Jenny. It was the same cabin, the same bed, and again it hadn't been slept in.

She moved back on to the veranda, half expecting David to come out from his cabin as he had done last time. But David's door was firmly closed. She knew he always slept with it open so that he could feel the breeze. So he must already be at the clinic, she deduced. She'd better leave a message for him about Mark.

She made her way quickly to the clinic and stopped at the reception desk. Nurse Chang looked up from the report she was writing.

'May I help you, Sister?'

'Yes. When you see Dr Sanderson would you tell him that I'm worried about his brother. I went to his cabin and. . .'

'Just one moment, Sister,' Nurse Chang put in. 'Dr Sanderson's brother left on the morning helicopter.'

'But does Dr Sanderson know?' queried Melissa.

'Yes. He accompanied his brother to the helicopter pad and saw him off.'

I bet he did! Melissa thought angrily. Couldn't wait to get rid of him. 'Where exactly is Dr Sanderson?' she asked evenly.

'Dr Sanderson is in Mr Victor Linden's room...but he said he was not to be disturbed, Sister!'

Melissa heard the rising tone of Nurse Chang's voice, but she ignored her words as she hurried towards Victor's room.

She paused outside, taking a deep breath and planning exactly what she would say to David.

Through the door she heard David's raised voice. 'But she really believes it's true, Victor.'

Angrily Melissa pushed open the door. 'Of course I believe it's true. Don't involve poor Victor in your deceit, David. You can't get him to lie. He's already told me the truth.'

She realised that both David and Victor were staring at her with a look of dismay. There was an ominous silence for a few seconds before David moved towards her and stood towering above her, his eyes blazing angrily.

'We're not talking about you, Melissa. We're talking about Jenny. If you hadn't been listening at the keyhole...'

'I wasn't listening at the keyhole! I was on my way here to tell you that you had no right to pack poor Mark off this morning. I heard you shouting at him last night and...'

'Melissa, be quiet!'

David's authoritative voice rang out, and Melissa

stopped as she remembered their patient, sitting in his chair beside the window. She realised how dreadfully unprofessional she had been to go into a patient's room and behave like this. But Victor was so heavily involved in their lives that she had begun to think of him as an old friend.

'Victor, I'm so sorry,' she began as she moved away from David and crossed the room. Sitting down beside her patient at the window, she put out her hand. 'I didn't mean to upset you.'

She stopped speaking as she saw the slow smile spreading across Victor's face. He turned to look at David. 'Isn't it time you explained the situation?' he said.

David moved swiftly, perching on the edge of the bed and looking down at both of them with a deeply serious expression.

'Victor, if you only knew how I've longed to hear those words! If only you hadn't sworn me to secrecy...'

'David, I'm sorry. But I thought it was best for the baby to think that I was his father and...'

'Will someone *explain*?' Melissa cut in, her voice rising in frustration.

The two men looked at each other. 'You first, Victor,' David said.

'My dear, I believe I owe you an apology,' Victor began quietly. 'I told you that Jenny was pregnant when she married me. What I didn't tell you was that the baby's father was Mark.'

'Mark?' she repeated, staring wide-eyed from one to the other of the men. 'So that's why he looks like a young Sanderson!' She turned to look up at David. 'And you knew about this, David?'

David nodded, but it was Victor who went on with the story. 'David was the one who had to pick up the pieces when Jenny jilted Mark. As soon as she found out she was pregnant she knew she had to find herself a husband quickly. But she didn't want a penniless student like Mark. So she went to see David.'

Melissa saw the pain in David's eyes. 'What happened, David?' she asked, as if in a dream.

David glanced across at Victor and he nodded his assent. 'Tell her everything, David. It doesn't hurt any more.'

'Jenny threw herself at me,' David told her. 'But I told her she wasn't my type. I didn't even want to take her out for the evening, let alone sleep with her. I knew she'd been seeing Mark, so I asked her what she was up to. It was then she admitted she was pregnant and she wanted to get married. . .but not to Mark. She told me that I was the one she'd always wanted, that Mark was too young and inexperienced for her.' David drew in his breath sharply. 'I told her that if Mark still loved her she should marry him.'

Melissa waited. 'And what did she say?'

'She laughed in my face. She said that if I wouldn't have her she knew someone who would.'

Victor stirred in his chair. 'Let me explain the next bit, David. Jenny came to see me at the office, and to give the girl her due, she put her cards on the table and told me the whole story. I'd known her since she was a girl and felt a sort of avuncular affection for her. . .although she was always a handful as a child. I remember I was feeling a bit lonely after the death of my first wife, so Jenny's idea of a matrimonial partnership appealed to me. And I'd always wanted a son. . .but that was where I made my mistake. I shouldn't have insisted that we keep quiet about the baby. You see, I told Jenny that we must pass him off as my son. . .that she must never tell the real father. That was when she told me that his brother already knew.'

Victor leaned back against his chair and ran a hand over his forehead.

David leaned forward and said, 'Take it easy, old man; I think you need a rest.'

Victor flashed him a grateful smile. 'Why don't you explain the remainder of the story to Melissa? You don't need me to corroborate it any more. I'm sure she'll believe you now.'

David moved over to stand beside Melissa's chair. 'I think we'll leave Victor in peace. It's our story from now on.'

Melissa looked up into his dark, enigmatic eyes. She was beginning to see the light, but there were still a lot of questions to be explained.

She contained her curiosity until they were well away from the clinic, walking through the forest towards the beachside path. She had handed over her morning's work to Sister Watson and David had left Mike Brent in charge of the clinic, so they had a few hours to themselves.

She felt as if she were in a dream as she ran up the steps to her cabin. David was close behind her. Firmly, he closed the door and sat down on one of the cane chairs.

She sat down on the other, eyeing him warily.

'You're still not entirely convinced, are you?' he said softly. 'What do I have to do to make you trust me?'

'Just tell me the whole truth,' she said, in a dazed tone. 'You said you were talking about Jenny believing something was true. What is it she believes?'

He gave her a wry grin. 'We've come to realise that Jenny is suffering from a severe personality disorder. She lives in a world of dreams. When she wants something to be true she only has to think about it and, in her disturbed mind, it becomes a fact. Victor has been having her treated by a psychiatrist since soon after the birth of baby Paul.'

Melissa's eyes widened. 'But most of the time she seemed so rational!'

'That's one of the symptoms of this disorder. That's why these patients seem so plausible. She must have been in a lucid state when you told her that Mark was coming out here. It triggered off her memory and she remembered her affair with him. That was when she decided to go away before she would have to confront him. She could be very shrewd on occasions. At other times she was totally irrational. I remember one night, Victor sent for me and asked me to calm her down. She was becoming hysterical with him. He asked me to take her away and try to persuade her she couldn't live in the past. He told me to use whatever means I could think of to. . .'

David broke off as he saw the slow smile beginning to spread across Melissa's face. 'What's so funny?'

She shook her head. 'Nothing,' she said in a nonchalant tone, remembering the moonlit encounter she had witnessed on the clinic corridor. David telling Jenny she couldn't live in the past, giving her a gentle kiss on the forehead.

'And did you calm her down?' she asked innocently.

'Eventually.' He reached across and took hold of her hand.

It was the first contact they had made since their break-up the day before. The warmth of his fingers sent a welcome tingling sensation down her spine again.

'I think you're beginning to believe me,' he said softly.

'I think I am, but carry on from where Victor left off; what happened when he agreed to marry Jenny but insisted she keep quiet about the father of her baby?'

David gave a deep sigh. 'That involved one of the most difficult decisions of my life. Jenny came to tell me she was getting married, but told me that I must never tell Mark he was the father of her child. He must never know that she was pregnant by him. Then Victor came to see me and repeated the same request. I felt sorry for him and agreed. We struck up a friendship with each other and kept in touch over the last four years. It was Victor who introduced me to the consortium and gave me a recommendation to his board of directors.'

David's fingers tightened on Melissa's and she looked up enquiringly into his eyes.

'Victor's been a good friend,' he told her. 'He's a

much stronger character than he appears. He's one of those people who always puts himself last. But I think he's learned his lesson where Jenny is concerned. In the weeks he's been here I've persuaded him that he must take more care of himself. But after the birth of little Paul, when he first told me about Jenny's strange behaviour, I persuaded him to take her to a psychiatrist. He agreed on condition that it be kept secret. He forbade me to tell anyone that his wife was having psychiatric treatment—he didn't want people to think she was mad. It would have been so much easier if I could have confided in you about Jenny's mental health, but I couldn't go back on my promise to Victor.'

'Of course not; but tell me what happened before Paul was born. You made the decision not to tell Mark?' she prompted.

'It wasn't lightly made, because I knew he was hopelessly infatuated by Jenny, the older woman in his life. I remember he came home on the night that Jenny called round with her request for secrecy. It was a Tuesday night, the night when Mark always went out with some of his fellow medical students. Jenny knew that he usually stayed out until midnight. Well, on this particular night, he'd decided to come home to do some revision for his exams.'

'So what did he do when he found Jenny alone with you?'

David took a deep breath. 'Everything would have been all right if Jenny hadn't put on one of her silly acts. She ignored Mark when he came in and started to insinuate that I'd invited her round. I asked her to leave. Mark went to the door and she told him she never wanted to see him again, that she'd fallen for someone else. . . Mark saw red! He came back into the room after Jenny had gone and. . .oh, it was so awful! I could only deny what she'd said, but I wasn't free to explain the situation to him.'

'Just as you weren't free to explain the situation to me,' said Melissa, feeling the weight lifting from her shoulders. 'But what's made it possible to explain to me now?'

'Yesterday, when you told me that Victor had admitted to you that he wasn't Paul's father, I knew that finally he'd come round to my way of thinking. I'd been trying to persuade him that if Mark could be told the truth and if he could meet up with Jenny again we might go a long way towards solving my own complicated love life. Today, I told him that I'd had enough of evading the issue. I was in danger of losing you. . .'

'You're right about that,' Melissa agreed. 'I'd made all the plans for my escape. When I heard you having a row with Mark last night it only helped to spur me on to action. I almost came round to join Mark's side.'

David smiled. 'I wish you had! We didn't row for long. Mark was furious at first, but then he became excited at the prospect of seeing his son.'

'But will Victor agree to that?'

David nodded. 'He's written a letter to Jenny's psychiatrist explaining the whole situation. He's going home soon to be with Jenny, but just in case Mark arrives first. . .'

'Mark is going to see Jenny?'

'Under medical supervision. Jenny's been taken

into psychiatric care since her arrival in England. I telephoned her psychiatrist when she left Changi Airport and arranged that he would meet her at Heathrow.'

'Oh, I'm so sorry.' For the first time, Melissa began to feel some sympathy for her old friend.

'She's in good hands,' said David. 'The psychiatrist suggested that it would be beneficial if she were to see Mark again. She might remember what really happened. At the moment she really believes her own story is true.'

'That's what you were explaining to Victor when I overheard you,' she said. 'And I thought you were talking about me. But isn't there a danger that Mark will fall in love with Jenny when he sees her again?'

David laughed. 'Mark's a pretty level-headed young man now. I realised that when I talked to him last night. He got over Jenny a long time ago. The thing he couldn't get over was the fact that he thought I'd double-crossed him. We had a great reunion last night when he understood what had really happened. But he readily agreed to go back to England when I offered him a ticket. I've asked him to see Jenny's psychiatrist and help in any way he can. He's also going to call in on Victor when he gets back next week so that he can see young Paul. Mark's quite happy to assume the role of family friend. He doesn't want to take Paul away from Victor, just to see him occasionally. He says he hopes to have his own family later on. . .when he's finished his medical studies.'

'He's going back to medical school?'

'He's going to try to get a place for next year. I've arranged to help him financially.'

Melissa laughed. 'Some row you had last night! When it went quiet I thought one of you had stormed off.'

'That was when we opened a bottle of champagne and agreed to put the past behind us. . .but Mark made one condition.'

'And what was that?'

'He wants to be best man at our wedding.'

'What wedding?'

'The wedding of the year! Surely you must have heard about it! It's going to take place on an idyllic island off the coast of Malaysia. It's an absolute tropical paradise!'

'You've got a nerve, Dr Sanderson! What makes you think I'd want to be led to the altar by a man who's done nothing but lead me up the garden path?'

'Because you love me. . .and I love you.'

He stood up, scooping her into his arms and carrying her over to the bed.

She felt the sensual arousal deep inside her. As he took her into his arms she knew that this time it would be different. Because he'd told her he loved her! The past was behind them, the present was idyllic and they were going to have a future together.

She moved in his arms. 'Will you say that again?'

'I love you,' he whispered. 'I love you. I always have and I always will.'

Mills & Boon

— MEDICAL ROMANCE —

The books for your enjoyment this month are:

AND DARE TO DREAM Elisabeth Scott
DRAGON LADY Stella Whitelaw
TROPICAL PARADISE Margaret Barker
COTTAGE HOSPITAL Margaret O'Neill

♥ ♥ ♥ ♥ ♥

Treats in store!

Watch next month for the following absorbing stories:

CROCK OF GOLD Angela Devine
SEIZE THE DAY Sharon Wirdnam
LEARNING TO CARE Clare Mackay
FROM SHADOW TO SUNLIGHT Jenny Ashe

Available from Boots, Martins, John Menzies, W.H. Smith, Woolworths and other paperback stockists.

Also available from Mills and Boon Reader Service, P.O. Box 236, Thornton Road, Croydon, Surrey CR9 3RU.

Readers in South Africa — write to:
Independent Book Services Pty, Postbag X3010, Randburg, 2125, S. Africa.

While away the lazy days of late Summer with our new gift selection
Intimate Moments

Four Romances, new in paperback, from four favourite authors.
The perfect treat!

The Colour of the Sea
Rosemary Hammond

Had We Never Loved
Jeneth Murrey

The Heron Quest
Charlotte Lamb

Magic of the Baobab
Yvonne Whittal

Available from July 1991. Price: £6.40

Mills & Boon

Available from Boots, Martins, John Menzies, W.H. Smith, Woolworths
and other paperback stockists.

Also available from Mills and Boon Reader Service,
P.O. Box 236, Thornton Road, Croydon, Surrey CR9 3RU.

Mills & Boon

Do you long to escape to romantic, exotic places?

To a different world – a world of romance?

THE PAGES OF A MILLS & BOON WILL TAKE YOU THERE

Look out for the special Romances with the FARAWAY PLACES stamp on the front cover, and you're guaranteed to escape to distant shores, to share the lives and loves of heroes and heroines set against backgrounds of faraway, exotic locations.

There will be one of these special Romances every month for 12 months. The first is set on the beautiful island of Tobago in the Caribbean.

Available from September, 1991 at:

Boots, Martins, John Menzies, W.H. Smith, Woolworths and other paperback stockists.

Also available from Mills and Boon Reader Service, P.O. Box 236, Thornton Road, Croydon, Surrey CR9 3RU.

COMING IN SEPTEMBER

The eagerly awaited new novel from this internationally bestselling author. Lying critically injured in hospital, Liz Danvers implores her estranged daughter to return home and read her diaries. As Sage reads she learns of painful secrets in her mothers hidden past, and begins to feel compassion and a reluctant admiration for this woman who had stood so strongly between herself and the man she once loved. The diaries held the clues to a number of emotional puzzles, but the biggest mystery of all was why Liz had chosen to reveal her most secret life to the one person who had every reason to resent and despise her.

Available: September 1991. Price £4.99

W(*)RLDWIDE

From: Boots, Martins, John Menzies, W.H. Smith,
Woolworths and other paperback stockists.
Also available from Reader Service, Thornton Road,
Croydon Surrey, CR9 3RU